# Parfaits and Paramours – Pelican Cove Cozy Mystery Series Book 7

## By Leena Clover

D1739285

# Chapter 1

Jenny King maneuvered her van around a steep curve and climbed over a small hill. She was still in awe of this exclusive part of Pelican Cove. The island's wealthy residents had their estates in this part of town. Sprawling mansions, extensive grounds and private beaches were the norm here. So were sparkling swimming pools and an army of domestic staff.

"Can you turn the heat on, please?" Jenny's friend Heather Morse asked with a shiver.

Spring had come early to Pelican Cove, bringing warmer days. Flowers were beginning to bloom along Main Street, promising a riot of color in the coming weeks. But the temperature dropped as the sun crept closer to the horizon. A large mosaic of pinks and mauves was scattered across the March sky, heralding sunset.

Jenny fiddled with the temperature knob and muttered an oath. The van was a relic, rarely used unless Jenny had any deliveries or catering jobs. Jenny didn't remember the last time she had paid for a full tank of gas for the rundown vehicle.

"We're almost there, Heather," she said in a chiding tone. "I told you to wear a warm sweater."

"Why don't you fix the heat?" Heather asked with a pout. "At least get an estimate from the auto shop."

"I did that," Jenny sighed. "I need to replace the thermostat. It's going to cost more than this pile of junk is worth."

The two friends bickered as the sky darkened and the sun set on the horizon.

"Give it a rest, Heather," Jenny pleaded. "I need to catch my breath before Ada Newbury launches her list of complaints."

Ada Newbury was one of the richest women in Pelican Cove. The Newburys belonged to an elite class of the island's population, the Pioneers. Their ancestors had come to the island hundreds of years ago and had been one of the first settlers. People still murmured about how the Newburys had become rich overnight, thanks to sunken treasure. But no one could deny that the Newburys were now rich as Croesus.

"She won't," Heather dismissed. "She loves your food. Why do you think she's paying double to have you cater this party?"

Jenny's face broke into a smile. Her life had taken an unexpected turn. She couldn't believe people from far and wide came to Pelican Cove to visit her café and gorge on her delicious food.

Jenny King had been a suburban soccer mom for most of her life. One day, her husband of twenty years had come home with devastating news. He was going out with a much younger girl who was now in the family way. He asked Jenny to clear out.

Jenny had sought shelter on the remote island of Pelican Cove. Her aunt, Star, had welcomed her warmly and opened her house and heart to Jenny. After letting her mope and sulk for a few weeks, Star had cajoled Jenny into starting work at her friend Petunia's café. The rest, as they said, was history.

Jenny had started working her magic in the kitchen and now the whole town of Pelican Cove was singing her praises. People lined up to taste her food. Jenny didn't disappoint, coming up with delicious new recipes every few days, using the area's abundant local produce and fresh seafood.

She had built a new life for herself on the island. She had made lasting friendships and found something she had never imagined she would have in her life again. Jenny King was in love.

Instead of settling into the mid forties' drudgery she thought was her lot in life, Jenny was writing a new chapter in her life.

"Do you think we have enough food?" Jenny asked Heather worriedly.

Ada Newbury had been too busy to go over the menu with Jenny. She had just wanted it to be fresh and modern. Jenny wondered what that meant. She just hoped the dishes she had come up with would pass muster with the old harridan.

"Everyone's going to be licking their fingers, Jenny," Heather said loyally. "Just wait and see."

Jenny pulled up outside a set of massive iron gates. A security guard came out of a small cabin and waved at them.

"Are you from the Boardwalk Café?" he asked. "You are late."

He spoke curtly into his phone and the gates swung open.

"It's two minutes past six," Jenny cursed. "Plenty of time to set up."

Ada Newbury was throwing a party for her grandson. He was recently engaged to a girl from the city. Their impending nuptials were the talk of the town. No expense was being spared and the locals were vying for an invitation to the country club extravaganza the wedding promised to be. Ada had arranged the party in lieu of a wedding shower. She called it a meet and greet for both sides of the family.

Jenny drove her van to the back of the house. A

marquee had been set up on the lawn and linen covered tables stood ready for the food. A life sized ice sculpture depicting an embracing couple graced the centre of the lawn. Fairy lights were woven through the trees and large paper lanterns swayed in the breeze.

"This place looks beautiful," Jenny gushed.

"Ada hired a party planner from the city," Heather supplied. "The planner works with a city based caterer but Ada stuck to her guns. She wanted your food for this party."

A tall, slim woman stepped out on the porch before Jenny had a chance to reply.

"You're late," she complained. "I hope you got everything?"

"Don't worry, Mrs. Newbury," Jenny hastened to assure the woman. "It's all under control."

"It better be," Ada snapped. "The guests arrive at seven."

She turned toward Heather.

"Your grandmother is here. We are having tea in the parlor."

Heather's grandmother and Ada Newbury were staunch rivals. Betty Sue Morse was formidable even in her eighties. She had been married to John Newbury, the older of the Newbury brothers. Amicably separated, she still blushed every time she came across the dapper old man.

Betty Sue was the descendant of the island's founder. It had been called Morse Isle then. Her family had originally owned the island. She was the fourth generation descendant of James Morse who had travelled south from New England with his family in 1837. He had bought the island for $125 and named it Morse Isle. He built a house for his family on a large tract of land. Fishing provided him with a livelihood, so did floating wrecks. He sent for a friend or two from up north. They came and settled on the island with their families. They in turn invited their friends. Morse Isle soon became a thriving community.

Being a barrier island, it took a battering in the great storm of 1962. Half the island was submerged forever. Most of that land had belonged to the Morse family. A new town emerged in the aftermath of the storm and it was named Pelican Cove.

Betty Sue had retained the Morse name even after her marriage. Heather was the last Morse on the island. Single at thirty five, she was a source of constant worry for her grandmother. Betty Sue wasn't ready to let the Morse bloodline end with Heather.

The Newburys and their money could not compete

with Betty Sue's pedigree. She made sure Ada knew that every time they met.

"I'm going to help Jenny set up here," Heather told Ada.

Ada shrugged, the look she directed at Heather full of disdain.

"Don't forget you are a guest here, Heather," she said, giving Jenny a withering look.

"She's right, Heather," Jenny said hastily. "Why don't you go meet Betty Sue? I can take it from here."

Heather mouthed a brief apology as she followed Ada inside the house.

The food was being served buffet style. Jenny worked quickly, aided by some of Ada's domestic staff and stood back to admire the lavish spread. She had taken different tastes into account and believed there was something for everyone.

The guests started trickling in at seven.

Ada leaned on a short, stocky young man with cobalt blue eyes. Jenny surmised he was the grandson.

Heather sipped cold soup from a small glass and sighed with pleasure.

"These gazpacho shots are genius!"

Jenny smiled proudly and looked around. Guests were exclaiming over the food, smacking their lips and going for seconds.

Ada walked over to Jenny.

"Do we have any crab dip?" she asked.

Jenny pointed toward a chunky dip resting in a sourdough bowl. It nestled on a platter with an assortment of crackers.

"Brandon loves it," Ada said, walking toward it.

She didn't bother to introduce Jenny to her grandson. Jenny was the help after all.

"That's Brandon," Heather whispered in her ear. "He's got a big job in the city, aide to some senator. His parents are proud of him."

"Where are they?" Jenny asked, looking around.

She had never set eyes on Ada's offspring before.

"Brandon's parents are on a world tour," Heather told her. "They have been on a cruise for six months. They are expected back before the wedding."

"And where's the bride?"

A short brunette with highlighted hair and violet eyes walked up to Jenny just then. Jenny found herself smiling back as the girl beamed at her. Jenny secretly admitted she envied the girl her youth and beauty.

"Your food is simply super," the girl gushed. "I can't have enough of that beer boiled shrimp. That cocktail sauce has just the right zing. And the caprese bites and the olive tapenade! A couple of my friends are vegetarian and they are amazed at all the veggie options. They thought they would have to starve here, you know."

Jenny thanked the girl politely.

"Meet the bride," Heather said, hugging the girl. "Kelly, this is my friend Jenny. She's the genius behind this whole spread."

Kelly popped a pimento cheese sandwich in her mouth and wiped her hand before extending it toward Jenny.

"I'm Kelly Fox," she said simply. "This is a wonderful party. Brandon's grandma is so cute, isn't she?"

Jenny stifled a smile. No one had ever called Ada Newbury 'cute'.

"She wanted the best for you," Jenny nodded. "I hope you enjoy your wedding shower."

A tall, brown haired man walked up to Kelly and put

an arm around her. His other hand held a glass of champagne. He threw back his drink and picked up a canapé from a tray.

"This is delicious," he said.

"Hummus and cucumber bites," Kelly read off the label. "Please tell me you are going to cater my wedding too."

"Who's this hunk?" Heather asked with a wink, staring at the tall and attractive stranger.

"Oh," Kelly cried. "Where are my manners? This is Binkie, my cousin. I'm an orphan, you see. I grew up in foster homes. Binkie is the only family I have here."

They chatted with Jenny and Heather and tasted everything on the buffet.

"Those turkey and avocado wraps are to die for," Binkie sighed. "You have a gift!"

"Save room for dessert," Jenny warned them. "We have banana mascarpone parfaits, and chocolate chip marshmallow cookies with ice cream."

Betty Sue Morse came over and chatted with Jenny.

"You've done a fine job here, girl," she said approvingly. "That crab dip is better than mine. And the shrimp is cooked just right."

Brandon came over with a ravishing beauty on his arm. She was shorter than Kelly but equally attractive. Her hazel eyes picked up the green in her dress and her carrot hair glistened in the soft light. Jenny was surprised the bride and groom weren't plastered to each other.

"Did you make those pimento cheese sandwiches?" the girl asked Jenny. "They are so yum! Everything is. I'm taking plenty of photos."

"Hello Megan," Heather said stiffly. "Didn't know you were in town."

"Brandon's getting married," Megan said brightly. "I wouldn't miss it for the world."

# Chapter 2

A sunny spring morning dawned in Pelican Cove. Jenny had arrived at the Boardwalk Café at 5 AM. She baked her signature muffins and assembled a dozen parfaits. Jenny's baking had taken a toll on her. She had gained at least twenty pounds in the two years since she had started dishing out her treats at the cafe. Personally, she preferred this slightly plump version of herself. She was certainly happier than she had been when she agonized over every leaf of lettuce she consumed. But she needed to fit into a wedding dress soon. This desire had inspired her to come up with healthier food options at the café. She was still experimenting with the perfect recipe for a berry yogurt parfait. Initial response had been encouraging.

Jenny's aunt Star arrived at the café around eight, looking sleepy. She guzzled a big cup of coffee and shooed Jenny out of the kitchen.

"Aren't you getting late? Don't give that shrew any more reason to yell at you."

Jenny needed to go back to the Newbury mansion to collect her stuff.

"I feel bad, making you work on a Saturday."

"Don't be silly," Star dismissed. "Most of the food is

already prepped. I can handle the café for a couple of hours."

Jenny got into her van and hummed a tune as she drove down the familiar road. She wondered when the party broke up the previous night. She had stuck on until nine the previous evening, refilling the food as needed. Her work was done once she finished serving the dessert.

"You may go now," Ada had told her curtly. "Come back tomorrow morning to clear up."

Jenny took the hint and drove home to rest her aching feet. She had spied Heather chatting with the bride in the distance. Heather was going to drive home with her grandmother.

The security guard in the cabin didn't come out this time. The iron gates opened and Jenny drove through, smiling back as the guard waved at her.

Jenny was relieved to see she didn't have much to do. Ada's staff had done the bulk of the work. Her large serving trays and dishes had been washed and dried and stacked on a table. All she needed to do was load the stuff in her van and be on her way. She looked around for her giant punch bowl and spotted it under the table.

Heather came out on the porch.

"Need a hand with that?"

"Heather!" Jenny exclaimed. "Did you stay over?"

"Grandma and I were right behind you. Brandon invited me for breakfast. He wants to properly introduce me to Kelly."

"You hardly need an introduction from what I saw."

"Kelly's a friendly soul," Heather nodded. "We hit it off last night. But Brandon sounded so eager. I'll let him show her off."

Brandon came out of the house. His face lit up when he saw Jenny.

"Your food was amazing. Kelly can't stop raving about it."

Jenny thanked him politely and took her leave.

"Why don't you stay for breakfast?" Brandon asked. "Kelly wants to talk to you about catering the wedding."

"Your grandma might have some other plans for that," Jenny said.

"Don't worry about Grandma," Brandon said confidently. "I can bring her around."

"Please stay," Heather pressed. "It will be fun."

Jenny knew Ada Newbury wouldn't be pleased. She hesitated.

"Why isn't Kelly here yet?" Heather asked Brandon. "Looks like she had a little too much champagne."

"Kelly's an early riser," Brandon said with a frown. "I'm going to call her."

He pulled a cell phone out of his pocket and turned around, jabbing some buttons on the screen.

"It's ringing," he explained.

A tall, strapping young man came running from the beach. Jenny sensed the panic in his coal black eyes. He came to a stop before Brandon and began gesticulating with his hands.

Brandon stared back at the youth in confusion.

"Get a grip, man!" Brandon exclaimed. "What's wrong with you?"

The man pointed somewhere behind him and started walking back.

"I guess he wants us to follow him," Heather muttered.

The youth whirled around and looked pleadingly at Heather.

"You wait," he stuttered.

He looked at Brandon.

"Come with me."

Brandon shrugged and began following the guy.

Heather raised her eyebrows and stared at Jenny.

"Who is he?" Jenny asked.

"The gardener?" Heather mused. "How would I know?"

A shout went up somewhere in the foliage behind Jenny. There was a flurry of footsteps and Brandon ran up to them, white in the face.

"It's Kelly," he cried, collapsing on the lawn.

He clutched his head in both hands as he stared wild eyed at Heather.

"She's dead. My Kelly's dead."

Ada Newbury came out on the porch.

"What's the commotion?" She gave Jenny a piercing look and stared at her grandson. "Why are you sitting on the grass, Brandon? Get inside. Cook's poaching the eggs for your Eggs Benedict."

Jenny found herself taking over. Ada refused to believe her grandson. She grabbed Heather by the hand and started walking through a gap in the trees. Jenny realized there was a small path there she hadn't noticed before. Heather and Ada were back a few minutes later. Heather gave a slight nod as she stared at Jenny. Jenny pulled out her phone and called the police.

Heather told her how they had found Kelly floating in the pool, face down. There was no doubt she had been dead for a while.

A wail of sirens sounded in the distance and grew louder as they approached the Newbury's mansion. The cook was coaxing Ada to drink a cup of tea. Jenny sat on a delicate chair with spindly legs, feeling out of place in the ornate parlor.

A tall, uniformed man came into the room, leaning on a cane. Jenny's heart sped up as she gazed into his piercing blue eyes. Adam Hopkins was the sheriff of Pelican Cove. He was also Jenny's betrothed. After a rocky courtship, Jenny had finally agreed to marry Adam the previous autumn. Six months later, they still hadn't set a wedding date.

"What are you doing here, Jenny?" Adam asked with a frown.

"I can't believe this is happening again," Ada Newbury wailed.

A stranger's corpse had been discovered on the Newbury estate several months ago.

"Did you know the deceased?" Adam asked stiffly.

He took his job seriously and was firmly in cop mode.

"Of course I did," Ada snapped. "My grandson was going to marry that girl."

"Where is he, by the way?"

Brandon had locked himself in his room. He had been inconsolable.

"That poor boy," Ada sobbed.

"When was the last time you saw this girl?"

Adam launched into a series of questions. Jenny knew the drill. Adam would be merciless in his questioning. He was just doing his job.

Adam let Jenny go after a few cursory questions. He warned her not to gossip about what had happened.

"Surely you know me better than that?" she fumed.

It was hard to keep anything secret in Pelican Cove. The Magnolias were waiting for Jenny back at the

Boardwalk Café. This was a motley group of women Jenny had grown fond of. She would lay her life down for one of them. Betty Sue Morse was the unopposed leader of the pack. Jenny's aunt Star was the most free spirited member of the group. Heather and Molly were the youngest. The Magnolias had suffered a shock the previous year when Petunia, their kindest member, had been struck down. They were still grieving for her. Petunia had left the Boardwalk Café in Jenny's care and she was doing everything she could to live up to her friend's legacy.

"Heather called," Betty Sue told Jenny, her hands busy knitting a canary yellow scarf.

"Is it true?" Molly asked, her eyes popping out of their Coke-bottle glasses.

Tall and scrawny, Molly worked at the local library and was hailed by her friends as one smart cookie.

"Do you know what happened?" Star asked Jenny.

Jenny looked thoughtful.

"That girl was brought up right," Betty Sue stated. "She asked after my arthritis. She even brought a wrap for me from inside."

Jenny remembered Kelly was an orphan. She wondered if anyone would grieve for her. She remembered the tall, handsome man who had been hanging around her. He had a funny name.

The Magnolias decided to stick around at the café until Heather got back. Jenny worked through the lunch crowd, trying to keep herself from calling Adam. He didn't appreciate personal calls when he was busy on the job.

"Time to have lunch," she told the Magnolias as she brought out a big platter of sandwiches.

The Magnolias sat on the deck of the café, overlooking the Atlantic Ocean. The bright sunlight was a bit deceptive as a cold wind whipped Jenny's tresses around her face.

The ladies were quiet as they munched on Jenny's chicken salad sandwiches. There was a big sigh of relief when they spotted Heather walking along the boardwalk toward them. She jogged up the café's steps and collapsed in a chair with a thud.

"I'm starving!" she complained. "I never had that breakfast."

Jenny fixed a plate for her while the others bombarded her with questions. Heather warded off their questions while she took a few bites. Then she delivered the shocking news.

"Ada Newbury has been arrested."

"That's outrageous!" Betty Sue declared. "Looks like your young man is up to no good again, Jenny."

"What was she arrested for?" Star asked Heather, ignoring Betty Sue.

"Kelly's murder."

"Isn't it too soon to say that?" Molly asked.

"Apparently not," Heather explained. "The police have decided that Kelly was murdered. And they think Ada had the strongest motive."

"That's a bit hasty, even for Adam," Jenny said reluctantly.

"Ada wasn't too fond of Kelly," Heather told them. "I think most of the staff knew that. She thought Brandon was marrying someone beneath him."

"So what's new?" Star asked, rolling her eyes. "Ada thinks everyone is beneath the Newburys."

"That's not a strong enough motive," Molly agreed.

"Adam must have had his reasons," Jenny said, coming to his defense.

"Does Julius know?" Betty Sue asked, referring to Ada's husband.

"Julius is out of town. He was going to call Jason when I left. I think Jason will bail her out soon."

Jason Stone was the one and only lawyer in Pelican Cove. He had known Jenny as a teen, when she had spent summers on the island visiting her aunt. He had tried to woo Jenny when she came to live in Pelican Cove again. Jenny was very fond of Jason but he hadn't made her heart race like Adam did. Jason still flirted with her at every possible opportunity and Jenny took it in her stride.

"Did you talk to that girl yesterday?" Star asked Jenny curiously.

"She was sweet," Jenny nodded. "And so pretty. No wonder Brandon fell for her."

Star exchanged a glance with Betty Sue.

"She was there," Betty Sue nodded cryptically. "The shameless hussy."

"Come on, Grandma," Heather grimaced. "That's all water under the bridge."

"What are you guys talking about?" Jenny asked them.

"Just some gossip," Heather dismissed. "Pay no heed, Jenny."

"Are they talking about Megan?" Molly asked.

"Isn't that the redhead Brandon was walking around with last night?" Jenny asked. "Who is she?"

# Chapter 3

Betty Sue clammed up at Jenny's question. Molly began to look uncomfortable. Heather took pity on Jenny and spoke up.

"Megan Patterson used to be Brandon's girl friend."

Jenny's mouth hung open.

"He seemed pretty friendly with her last night."

"Megan dumped him," Heather explained. "I wonder if Brandon still has a thing for her."

Jenny's opinion of Brandon took a nosedive.

"You don't say? Did Kelly know about their past?"

Heather shrugged.

"How would I know?"

Betty Sue rushed to Brandon Newbury's defense.

"Brandon's a good boy. He turned out pretty well, considering."

"Why don't you tell her the whole story?" Star suggested.

"Ada and Julius adore Brandon," Heather supplied. "Ada as good as raised him. He spent a lot of his childhood here."

"What about his parents?" Jenny asked.

"They like to travel," Betty Sue grunted. "They are off gallivanting in some little known country most of the time. They never had time for Brandon."

"What does this have to do with Megan?" Jenny asked, wondering if there was a point to the conversation.

"Megan's grandparents live here too," Star explained. "She did some of her schooling here. She was a popular girl, head of the cheerleading squad and all that."

"So Megan and Brandon met years ago?"

"They are childhood sweethearts," Heather sighed. "It's hard to forget that kind of history."

"What does this Megan do?" Jenny asked.

"She lives in the city," Heather explained. "I have no idea what she does. No one knows what went wrong between her and Brandon."

"They must have made up though," Molly spoke. "Why would he invite her otherwise?"

"Ada threw last night's party, remember?" Betty Sue said. "Maybe Ada invited Megan."

"Let me guess," Jenny smirked. "Ada actually likes this girl?"

"She's besotted by her," Heather corrected. "Very few people can gain Ada's favor. Megan's one of them. She's always been welcome at the Newbury mansion."

Jenny wondered if Ada had been trying to mend fences between Megan and Brandon.

"What sort of man is Brandon?" Jenny asked. "Would he leave Kelly in the lurch if Megan went back to him?"

"Men!" Star spat. "Who can predict what they will do?"

"Brandon's not like that," Heather argued. "He really loved Kelly."

"Where did he meet her?" Jenny asked.

"We were going to talk about that this morning," Heather said. "I guess we won't be doing that anymore."

"Speaking of weddings," Betty Sue said. "When are you setting a date, Jenny?"

Jenny couldn't control the blush that stole over her.

"I haven't thought about it yet."

"You have had six months to think about it," her aunt reminded her. "You have to stop dilly dallying now."

"I can't wait to be a bridesmaid," Heather hinted.

"I thought Chris and Molly might beat me to it," Jenny said, trying to divert attention from herself.

Molly obliged them by turning red. She was dating Chris Williams, a young local realtor. Molly and Chris had exchanged promise rings a few months ago, instead of engagement rings. They both wanted to be completely sure of their commitment to each other before assigning any labels to their relationship.

"We are not in a hurry," she said quickly. "I think you and Adam should take the plunge first, Jenny."

Heather looked at them irritably.

"You are both one of a kind. You know what I would be doing if I was in your place? I would be knee deep in wedding magazines and stuff, planning the wedding of the century. And here you can't even set a date."

"Don't forget, Heather," Jenny said gently. "Adam and I have both been married before."

"So have I," Molly reminded her.

Neither of their marriages had ended well.

"So what?" Heather rolled her eyes. "This is a new beginning for both of you. Forget those losers you were married to before. Adam and Chris are some of the finest men you could ever meet."

"I fully agree with that," Jenny said with a laugh.

"What's holding you back then, sweetie?" Star asked, looking worried.

Jenny rubbed the tiny gold heart shaped charm that hung around her neck. She did that whenever she thought of her son Nick. Nick had gifted her a gold charm every Mother's Day ever since he turned eight. Jenny wore them all on a chain now. They provided her a tangible connection with her son whenever she thought of him.

"What does Nick feel about this?" Molly asked, picking up on Jenny's thoughts.

"We've never really discussed it," Jenny confessed.

"It's high time you did," Star quipped. "Nick is a grown man. He just wants you to be happy."

Jenny humored the Magnolias as they pestered her about her wedding. The group finally broke up when

Molly got up to get back to the library. Heather and Betty Sue returned to the Bayview Inn to prepare for the arrival of their new guests.

Star stayed back to help Jenny.

"When are you going to hire some help?" she asked Jenny. "You've been running the café singlehandedly for over six months now. It's taking a toll on you."

Jenny barely heard her aunt. She had been ignoring her aching back and sore feet for several weeks now. She couldn't explain why she hadn't hired some permanent staff for the café. The truth was she still missed her friend Petunia. Hiring someone else felt like she was replacing her. Jenny couldn't imagine doing that.

Jenny drove home as the daylight waned early under a cloudy sky. Her phone rang moments after she collapsed on the couch in her great room.

It was Adam, asking her what kind of food she fancied that evening. She had completely forgotten their dinner date.

Jenny showered and slipped into her trusty little black dress. She wished she had something new and bright to wear. Maybe she needed a shopping trip with the girls.

Adam was right on time. Jenny had a hankering for Mexican food. Adam drove to a small Mexican restaurant in a neighboring town.

Adam was in a sober mood.

"She was barely 25, Jenny," he moaned, referring to Kelly Fox. "She had her whole life ahead of her."

"Are you sure she didn't drown by herself?" Jenny asked hesitantly. "The champagne was flowing freely last night."

"I'm sure," Adam said. "We'll know more after the autopsy. But I am pretty sure someone killed that girl."

"But why?"

"That's what I have to find out."

Adam took a hefty bite of his taco and chewed thoughtfully. Jenny recognized the grim determination in his eyes.

"She seemed very happy," Jenny supplied. "Who wouldn't be? Brandon Newbury is supposed to be a great catch."

"Ada Newbury didn't like her," Adam said flatly. "Almost every member of their staff told me that."

"Did they have an argument or something?"

"Ada warned her off. Told her no good would come of marrying Brandon."

"Is that why you arrested her?"

"I didn't arrest her, Jenny," Adam sighed. "You have to stop listening to the grapevine. I just brought her in for questioning."

"Why does she need a lawyer then?" Jenny pounced. "You are hiding something from me."

Normally, Jenny's statement would have produced an outburst from Adam. But he had mellowed a bit since their engagement.

"I don't have to tell you everything I know, Jenny," he said with a smile. "I can't. It's part of an ongoing investigation."

"How did you zero in on Ada so quickly?" Jenny pressed. "Doesn't she have an alibi?"

Adam and Jenny parried back and forth, Jenny trying hard to squeeze as much information as possible from Adam. They shared a caramel flan for dessert and Adam took her to their favorite beach. Jenny forgot all about the Newburys as she held hands with Adam. They walked silently in the bright moonlight, enjoying each other's company.

Jenny started the next day with a smile on her face. She beamed at her favorite customer, the first in line when she opened the Boardwalk Café for business every morning. Captain Charlie gave her a knowing look.

"How's that young man of yours?" he asked. "I hear he hasn't thrown a tantrum in three full days."

Adam Hopkins was known for his irascible nature. Everyone believed Jenny had succeeded in taming him.

"Adam's fine, Captain Charlie," Jenny sighed. "Are you going to try one of my yogurt parfaits today? You need to start eating healthy."

Captain Charlie agreed to try Jenny's fancy breakfast, provided he could still eat his muffin. Jenny packed a blueberry muffin for him along with the berry parfait.

Most of the café's customers turned out to be like Captain Charlie. They went for the parfait only after they had their fill of muffins and omelets, treating the parfait as dessert.

"Does anyone here understand the concept of a low calorie breakfast?" Jenny wailed.

"I don't see why you are complaining," Star laughed. "More business for you."

"I thought I would help build some healthy habits," Jenny said reproachfully.

"That's a noble thought," Star said sagely. "But it ain't happening here, Jenny. The people in this town are set in their ways. You should know that by now."

After a dozen more customers chose a crab omelet over the parfait, Jenny had to admit her aunt was right. Jenny brainstormed about how she could make her parfaits more attractive.

"What if I add toasted coconut, or pecans?"

"Or chocolate chips?" her aunt suggested naughtily.

The Magnolias arrived at ten for their daily coffee break. Heather and Molly dutifully ate a parfait each while Betty Sue stuck to her muffin.

"You might be getting a visitor today," Heather told Jenny.

A long, black car pulled up outside the café just then. A uniformed driver got out and opened the back door. Ada Newbury stepped out, resplendent in a silk dress and a thick strand of pearls. Her head was held high and her expression was as haughty as ever. She stepped into the café and walked out on the deck.

"You there," she called out, snapping her fingers at Jenny.

Jenny didn't appreciate being insulted in her own café. She stood her ground, barely budging an inch.

"What can I do for you, Mrs. Newbury?"

"We need to talk."

Jenny invited her to pick an empty table. Ada's lips curled in an expression of disgust. She pulled out a lace handkerchief from her purse and placed it on a deck chair. She sat down gingerly, flicking a speck of dust off her sleeve.

Jenny sat down before Ada and folded her hands. She raised her eyebrows questioningly and waited for Ada to speak up.

"Your young man has gone berserk."

Jenny was silent, waiting for Ada to say more.

"He thinks we killed that silly girl."

"Did you?" Jenny asked.

"How dare you!" Ada fumed. "Brandon was in love with her."

"But you didn't like her, did you?" Jenny asked.

"She was a nobody," Ada spat. "Brandon could have done so much better."

"Looks like you don't have to worry about her now," Jenny said with a shrug.

"How I wish that were true," Ada said.

Her posture seemed to crumple and she suddenly

looked frail and old.

"Why are you here, Mrs. Newbury?" Jenny asked. "Are you here to complain about the food at the party?"

Ada looked pathetic as she leaned forward and grasped Jenny's arm.

"I need your help. Find out who killed that girl. I will pay you anything you want."

"I'm not a detective," Jenny protested. "And I don't want your money."

"Then take pity on me," Ada pleaded. "I'm innocent. I may have disliked that girl, but I didn't do anything to harm her."

"I can't guarantee anything," Jenny sighed.

Ada's voice wavered as her eyes bore into Jenny's.

"Just promise me you'll look into it."

# Chapter 4

Adam and Jenny were having an old argument. Adam was incensed as he cut into his eggs.

"I don't see why you have to be involved this time."

"Ada Newbury needs my help. She personally came over here and begged me to help her."

"That's convenient," Adam jeered. "Have you forgotten how that woman treats you most of the time? What about the way she snubs your aunt?"

"I know all that. And I am also sure she won't change even if I manage to bail her out of trouble."

"Then why are you bending over backwards, meddling in police business?"

"Don't forget I have helped you out in the past," Jenny said. "And I don't meddle. You do your thing. I'll do mine."

"Things are different now, Jenny. People know about us. They will assume I tell you everything about the investigation."

Jenny let out a snort.

"You're not giving out any state secrets, Adam. And here I thought you were worried about my safety."

Adam had the grace to look a bit guilty.

"Of course I worry about you. I haven't forgotten all those close calls you have had in the past couple of years, Jenny. What would I do if something happened to you?"

Jenny poured a fresh cup of coffee for Adam and rolled her eyes.

"You're making too much out of this."

Adam shook his head in disgust. He and Jenny agreed about most things. But he couldn't curb her sleuthing. Jenny called it helping people. He called it poking her nose into someone else's business.

"Time to go," Adam said, pushing his chair back and struggling to his feet.

He was a war veteran who had been injured in the line of duty. He had a pronounced limp and needed a cane most of the time. His recent therapy had led to a lot of improvement though. He was secretly hoping to get through his wedding without the cane. It was supposed to be a surprise for Jenny.

Jenny waved goodbye to Adam and went inside. She hadn't told him about her plans for the day.

Star was chopping vegetables in the kitchen.

"I will get the soup started before I leave," Jenny told her. "I should be back in time for lunch."

She started sautéing vegetables in a knob of butter.

"Are you going alone?" Star asked.

Jenny nodded. She usually took Heather along with her for moral support. But she had to stop being in awe of the Newburys at some point.

Bright blue skies studded with fluffy white clouds brought a smile to Jenny's face. Watery sunlight bathed everything in a soft glow as Jenny drove to the Newbury estate. She handed over a bag of muffins to the security guard at the gate. He thanked her profusely, looking surprised.

A maid ushered Jenny into the opulent living room. Jenny stood in the center of the room, looking around, wondering where to sit.

"Are you going to stand there all day?" Ada Newbury griped, snapping at Jenny as she came in.

The maid entered with a tray loaded with tea things. There was a three tiered stand with tiny cakes and cookies, and a big kettle of tea.

Ada poured tea for them and added milk and sugar to

Jenny's cup. Jenny wasn't sure if Ada remembered how she took her tea, or she just assumed.

"Try the shortbread," Ada said. "It's our cook's specialty."

Jenny obliged her and bit into the buttery, crumbly cookie.

"Let's talk about Megan," she said.

Ada looked surprised.

"Did you invite her to the party?" Jenny cut to the chase.

Ada nodded.

"Did Brandon ask you to do that?"

"I don't think he knew Megan was in town."

"I'm guessing you had something to do with that too," Jenny asked.

"Megan is such a sweet girl," Ada sighed. "She and Brandon always got along like a house on fire."

"But Brandon was seeing someone else," Jenny reminded her. "He was engaged to Kelly."

"Megan used to be here all the time, running after Brandon. She would come here after school. They would do their homework together and beg Cook for more fruit cake."

Ada sounded wistful as she reminisced about years gone by.

"What did you hope to achieve by inviting Megan?"

"Megan works in the city too," Ada said. "I told her to come down to Pelican Cove this weekend. This was her last chance if she wanted to win Brandon back."

Jenny was confused.

"I heard she was the one who left Brandon."

"Girls are fickle at that age," Ada dismissed. "I think they had a lovers' tiff. Megan must have thought Brandon would beg her to take him back. I think her plan backfired."

"Do you know this for a fact or are you just guessing?"

Ada's face slipped into a familiar haughty expression.

"I have seen a lot more of life than you have, young lady. That girl loves my Brandon. I am sure about that."

"So you were hoping that she and Brandon would get back together this weekend?"

Ada was silent but Jenny had her answer.

"What about the wedding? I thought it's all planned out."

"Plans can be canceled," Ada said harshly. "Marriage is for life. You know what they say, marry in haste, repent at leisure." Ada gave Jenny a calculating look. "I'm sure you have first-hand experience with it."

Nasty Ada was back.

"I was happy with my husband," Jenny said lamely, then gave up.

Ada Newbury would probably hold her responsible for her philandering husband.

"Never mind that," Ada quipped. "Brandon completely forgot how happy he was with Megan. He needed a reminder."

"So you asked Megan to come to Pelican Cove. Was she in on your plan to drive a wedge between the happy couple?"

Ada shrugged.

"Megan's a smart girl. I was sure she would figure it out."

"Was Brandon surprised to see Megan at the party?"

"He was overjoyed. I can tell you that. He clung to her all evening."

Jenny remembered how she had mistakenly thought that Megan was Brandon's betrothed. Brandon may not have been in love with her, but he clearly still adored her. They must have remained friends even after their breakup, Jenny mused. Maybe they had continued to meet. They did live in the same city.

"What did Kelly think about it?"

"I don't know. I was hoping she would be angry."

"Did you think she would create a scene?" Jenny probed.

Ada blushed.

"She hid her reaction, whatever it was. She seemed cool with Megan. I can't understand these youngsters. In my day, I would never have tolerated an interloper. I would have gauged her eyes out."

Jenny realized the opposite had happened.

"Kelly is the victim here, Mrs. Newbury," she reminded Ada. "Not Megan. Looks like you don't have to worry about Brandon marrying Kelly now."

"I didn't want her dead," Ada sighed. "I just wanted her to leave my grandson alone."

"Why didn't you like Kelly?" Jenny asked, genuinely curious. "She was pretty enough."

"The Newburys can trace their roots back to the Mayflower. Who was this girl, an orphan? She had no idea who her family was."

"No one cares about that stuff now," Jenny said gently.

"We do," Ada said stiffly. "Bloodlines matter to us."

Jenny couldn't hold herself back.

"I suppose Megan has an impeccable bloodline."

"She'll do. She's not a Pioneer, but her family has lived here since the 19th century."

"Did you ever give Kelly a chance?" Jenny asked, exasperated. "She might have been a really nice person."

Ada didn't bother to reply.

"Do you think Megan was capable of harming Kelly?" Jenny asked.

"She didn't need to," Ada replied. "You were here. You saw how besotted Brandon was with her. Megan would have charmed her way into his heart anyhow."

"When did Megan go home that night?"

Ada wasn't sure. She had retired to her room around nine thirty, a few minutes after Jenny herself left. The party was in full swing at that time. Everyone had imbibed a bit too much by then. Jenny remembered seeing Megan giggling over something Brandon said.

"Where is Brandon?" Jenny asked. "Is he staying here with you?"

"Of course," Ada snapped. "This is his home."

"How is he handling this?"

"That poor boy! He hasn't come out of his room since yesterday."

Jenny realized she would have to talk to Brandon some other time. She didn't relish speaking to him in front of Ada anyway.

"Have the police contacted you again?" Jenny asked.

"The sheriff called just before you got here," Ada told her. "That girl died sometime around midnight. Someone bashed her head in, it seems."

Jenny wondered if Kelly had already been dead when she was pushed into the pool. She would have to beg Adam for more details.

"Can you think of anyone who might have wanted to harm Kelly?" she asked Ada.

Ada shook her head.

"I barely knew the girl. Honestly, I didn't make an effort to get to know her."

Ada's brow furrowed and she muttered under her breath. "She could have died somewhere else."

"I'm sure she didn't choose to be killed on your property, Mrs. Newbury," Jenny said lightly.

Ada paid no attention to Jenny's sarcasm. She suddenly leaned forward in her chair.

"I had a feeling about her, you know."

"You mean, like, an intuition?"

Ada's face hardened.

"She was wrong for my Brandon. She would have hurt him, I am sure."

"You do realize Kelly is the victim here?" Jenny said mildly.

"That doesn't mean she was blameless."

Ada seemed intent on painting Kelly as the villain. Jenny tried to get her to focus on the problem at hand.

"We need to figure out who had a grudge against Kelly," Jenny said patiently. "Who, other than you, hated her enough to take her life?"

Ada looked at her watch and stood up.

"We'll have to continue some other time. I have a golf lesson at the club."

"You play golf?" Jenny asked, surprised.

Ada Newbury didn't look like she would voluntarily break a sweat.

Ada's face lit up at the question.

"I never took an interest in golf, until a few weeks ago. We have the best golf pro at the country club. He says I have a natural flair for the game."

Jenny had once been an avid golfer herself. Her husband had insisted she learn the game so they could play couples' golf and hobnob with his rich clients. She reflected over how much her life had changed since then. She didn't miss the forced socializing but she yearned for a good game.

"I love golf," she said eagerly. "How about a friendly round sometime?"

Ada was kind in her dismissal.

"I'll think about it."

"I need to talk to everyone who was working here on the night of the party," Jenny told Ada, getting back to business.

"Just make sure you don't take them away from their duties," Ada warned.

"I will also need to talk to Brandon," Jenny reminded her.

"Brandon will contact you when he is ready," Ada said. "I will make sure of it."

"We'll talk again," Jenny nodded, taking her leave.

Jenny drove back to the Boardwalk Café, going over her conversation with Ada in her mind. She didn't think she had made any progress that day.

Jenny started helping her aunt make lunch as soon as she reached the café. Star had marinated the shrimp based on Jenny's instructions. Jenny's stomach rumbled with hunger as she fried the shrimp for po' boy sandwiches. She slathered her homemade tartar sauce on soft white rolls and thought about her next step.

She decided to talk to Megan. Now that Kelly was dead, Brandon was single again. Megan definitely had a lot to gain by Kelly's death.

# Chapter 5

The Magnolias were assembled in the kitchen of the Boardwalk Café. Jenny had woken up to a light drizzle and grey skies. The rain picked up after 9 AM, promising a wet day. The café's deck was soaked and Betty Sue had grudgingly agreed to sit inside.

"How well do you know this Megan?" Jenny asked Heather.

"I used to babysit her," Heather replied. "And we all know each other on the island."

"Her grandmother is in my knitting circle," Betty Sue added. "The Pattersons are a well respected family in Pelican Cove."

"Why is that important?" Jenny asked. "You sound just like Ada."

"Breeding will tell," Betty Sue said. "You youngsters don't realize it."

"I need to go talk to Megan," Jenny told them. "Can one of you come with me?"

Molly couldn't get away from her desk at the library.

"You know I'm your wing woman," Heather said

eagerly. "When do you want to go?"

"Give me half an hour," Jenny said.

She spent some time prepping for lunch. Star assured Jenny she could assemble the crab salad sandwiches when needed.

Heather knew where Megan lived and she also knew her phone number. Jenny made sure she was available to talk to them. The rain started coming down in torrents just when they got into her car.

Heather called out the directions. Jenny drove carefully, squinting at the water logged road. One of her wiper blades was broken and her car was due for an oil change. She had taken much better care of her vehicles when she lived in the city. Although she barely drove two miles a day now, her car was beginning to exhibit some wear and tear.

"What kind of person is Megan?" Jenny asked Heather. "Does she tend to fly off the handle?"

"Megan's a friendly girl," Heather said. "Don't be fooled by that red hair."

"She has quite a presence," Jenny nodded.

"She's always been popular," Heather told Jenny. "She kind of takes over everything. But people still like her."

Megan welcomed them with a wide smile and led them to a sun room that looked out on a beautiful garden.

"I'm here to help you any way I can," Megan said before Jenny had a chance to speak up. "Poor Brandon! He was crazy about Kelly."

"What did you think about her?" Jenny asked.

"Kelly was a sweetheart."

"You sound as if you knew her."

"Kelly and I got along really well," Megan explained. "We met a few months ago in the city. Brandon introduced us."

Jenny couldn't hide her surprise.

"You knew Brandon was engaged?"

"Of course," Megan said without any guile. "Brandon and I have been friends since we were barely out of braces. He tells me everything."

"Wasn't that odd?" Heather interrupted. "You two were an item after all."

Megan laughed. She sounded genuine.

"So what? We parted amicably. I always want the best for Brandon."

"Who invited you to the party?" Jenny asked her. "Did Brandon know you were coming?"

"He didn't. Kelly and I wanted to surprise him."

"Wait. Kelly knew you were coming?" Jenny couldn't hide her surprise. "I thought Ada Newbury invited you to the party."

"She's a dear, isn't she?" Megan gushed. "I let her think that. Kelly had already told me about the party."

"You spent a lot of time with Brandon there."

"It was just like old times," Megan said wistfully. "We caught up with all our friends."

"Kelly must have felt left out," Jenny suggested.

"Kelly didn't mind," Megan said confidently. "She wasn't clingy. Not like some girls I know."

Heather had been tapping her foot impatiently while Megan spoke. She interrupted them suddenly.

"Wait a minute, Megan. Are you actually saying you were friends with Kelly?"

Megan shrugged.

Jenny picked up the conversation.

"Looks like you knew Kelly Fox well enough. What

kind of a person would you say she was?"

Megan thought for a minute.

"I'm no judge of character. She seemed like a regular gal."

"Why would someone want to kill her?"

Megan looked stricken.

"Kill her? Are you saying someone deliberately murdered her?"

Jenny couldn't believe Megan was that naïve.

"You do live in Pelican Cove?" Heather asked Megan. "How do you not know this?"

"I've been busy catching up with work since yesterday," Megan said lightly. "I haven't really talked to anyone."

"What kind of job do you have in the city?" Jenny asked politely.

"I'm a publicist," Megan said proudly. "I have a long roster of clients who always need something. They keep me on my toes."

She looked at her watch.

"I have a video call with a client in half an hour. I really need to prep for it."

"Just a few questions more," Jenny smiled. "When did you leave the party?"

"Frankly, I have no idea!" Megan sighed. "I think I went a bit overboard with the champagne."

"How long did the party go on?"

Megan pursed her mouth, shaking her head from side to side.

"I can't tell you that either. But there were a few people milling about when I left."

"What about Kelly?" Jenny asked. "When did you last see her?"

"Kelly was having the time of her life," Megan said. She narrowed her eyes as if she was trying to remember what had happened at the party. "I remember telling her I was leaving. She wanted me to stay a bit longer."

"Did you?" Heather asked.

"I might have. I started to leave a couple of times. But then I stayed on. My memory is really hazy on that point."

"Do you know anyone who might have wanted to

harm Kelly?" Jenny asked Megan.

Megan shook her head.

"I didn't know much about her personal life. She was friendly but she didn't share much about herself. I thought it might be because she didn't have a family. I didn't want to pry."

Jenny couldn't think of any more questions to ask the girl.

"So it was just a regular party ... you didn't notice anything unusual."

"Not really," Megan said, getting up.

Heather and Jenny took the hint.

"Thanks for talking to us, Megan," Jenny said with a smile. "Will you call me if you think of anything else?"

"Sure," Megan nodded. "I know the party ended in disaster. But I really enjoyed your food. I could go for that crab dip any day."

"You should go to the Boardwalk Café," Heather told her. "Jenny cooks something different every day."

"Oh yeah," Jenny said. "Come over to the café any time. I'll make you anything you like."

Jenny and Heather went over their visit on the way back to the café.

"Don't you think she's a bit too chirpy?" Jenny asked.

"You think it's all an act?" Heather quirked an eyebrow. "This is how Megan is. She gets along really well with people."

"Maybe she just told us what we wanted to hear."

"Do you think she was lying, Jenny?"

"I know Megan belongs to a different generation," Jenny said, swerving to avoid a puddle. "But surely the world hasn't changed that much? Friends with Kelly? I don't buy that."

"She could have been leading us on," Heather mused. "But why would she do that?"

"To hide the truth, of course," Jenny said. "I say she hated Kelly. I am ready to wager anything on that."

"How are you going to prove that?" Heather asked.

Jenny didn't have an answer for that. Heather continued thinking out loud.

"Do you think she had a motive?"

"I think so," Jenny said. "Now that Kelly's out of the

way, she has a straight shot at Brandon."

"Don't forget she broke up with him."

"She might have realized her mistake after she lost him. I saw how possessive she was of Brandon at the party. She was a woman on the prowl, make no mistake."

"You may be right," Heather relented. "But I don't think she needed to kill Kelly to get Brandon back. Have you looked at Megan? She can bewitch any man in a five mile radius."

"Don't be ridiculous!" Jenny threw back her head and laughed.

Heather joined in. Jenny called her out on her tendency to exaggerate.

"But seriously," Heather said, "she has a silver tongue to match those looks. It's a lethal combination."

"She doesn't really have an alibi," Jenny pointed out. "And she's not ready to commit to when she left the party."

"Have the police questioned her yet?" Heather asked. "She will have to give them some concrete answer."

"Adam might get more out of her," Jenny agreed.

Megan would have to give an accurate account of her movements to the authorities. There would be repercussions if she lied to them. Jenny wondered if Megan had been spinning a yarn all along. Had she sweet talked Jenny into believing what she wanted her to believe?

"Who's next on your list, Jenny?"

"Brandon Newbury."

"I'm sure Brandon's innocent," Heather said. "And I'm not just saying that because we are related. Brandon couldn't hurt a fly."

"I want to talk to Ada's staff too. They will open up more if you are with me."

"We don't have too many bookings at the inn this week. I'm not busy."

"Great. Am I missing anyone else?" Jenny asked.

"You already talked to Ada," Heather said, counting off her fingers. "Megan and Brandon are the major players. Aren't you forgetting Kelly?"

"She can't talk to me, Heather," Jenny smirked.

Heather punched her in the shoulder.

"What do you know about Kelly, huh?"

Jenny realized what she had been missing. She clicked her tongue in annoyance.

"How could I forget that? We definitely need to find out more about Kelly. I'm going to do some basic online research tonight."

Jenny dropped Heather off at the Bayview Inn and headed to the Boardwalk Café. Her aunt had assembled a tray of sandwiches and was already serving them to the lunch crowd. Soup was simmering on the stove. Jenny pulled on an apron and joined her aunt, shrugging off her fatigue.

Jason Stone came in just as the café emptied. Tiny droplets of water streamed down his face. He wiped his face with a white linen handkerchief and smiled broadly at Jenny, opening his arms wide for a hug.

"How's my favorite café owner today?"

Jenny hugged him back.

"You need to dry your hair," she said.

She grabbed a bunch of paper towels from a table and led Jason out to the deck. Jason obliged her and dried his hair sheepishly.

"What a day! We have two more days of this infernal rain. I can't wait for the sun to shine again."

"My garden needs this rain," Jenny said. "I'm looking forward to a great flowering season."

Jason asked Jenny to join him for lunch.

"Go ahead, sweetie," Star said. "You gotta eat."

"What about you?" Jenny asked her aunt.

Star was an artist who painted seascapes of the surrounding region. They were popular with the tourists. She had put her work on hold to help Jenny at the café. Jenny knew her aunt was burning the midnight oil to keep up with the demand for her work. She was worried about her health.

"I'm going to grab a sandwich and eat it on my way home," Star told her.

"No way," Jenny protested. "Eat with us. You can go paint up a storm after that."

Star relented.

"How's that old grouch treating you?" Jason asked, taking a jab at Adam.

"Very well, thank you very much," Jenny said, making a face. "What about you? Are you seeing someone?"

Jason's face clouded over. He laughed nervously, trying to look stoic.

"I'm too busy to date," he told them. "I have so many pending cases, I am working 12 hour days to get through them."

Star gave him a knowing look. She knew Jason still had a thing for Jenny. Unfortunately, it didn't look like they had a future together.

# Chapter 6

Jenny and Heather were back at the Newbury estate. Heather exclaimed in delight the moment they stepped into the parlor.

A tall, stout man with a shock of white hair held his arms out to Heather. Heather ran into them and hugged the man tightly.

"How are you, munchkin?" the man asked.

Robert Newbury was Heather's grandfather. He and Betty Sue had been separated for decades.

"When did you get back home?" Heather asked him.

"Last night," Robert answered. "What's the matter with you kids? I leave town for a couple of days and you manage to land in hot water."

"You know," Heather murmured. "How is Brandon?"

"Still crying his eyes out. I don't blame him, of course. There are some times in life when a man should not be ashamed of showing his emotions."

"We were hoping to talk to him," Jenny spoke up.

"You remember my friend Jenny?" Heather asked her

grandpa. "She's helping us find out what happened to Kelly."

Robert's face fell.

"That Kelly. She was a sweet girl. She was good for Brandon."

Jenny noticed how his opinion was diametrically opposite to that of Ada's.

"We are here to talk to the staff," Heather told her grandfather. "Can I catch up with you later?"

"Stay for lunch," Robert urged. "Cook's making fried chicken with all the fixings."

Heather promised him she would think about it. Jenny curbed an urge to giggle. She couldn't imagine Ada Newbury inviting her to eat lunch with the family.

Heather led Jenny down a long passage. She pushed open a door and entered a cavernous kitchen. A large woman wearing a chef's hat and a soiled apron around her wide girth stood with one arm on her hip, frying chicken. Her face broke into a broad smile when she looked up and spotted Heather.

"Hey baby girl! Come taste some bread pudding. I made that special brandy sauce you like."

Heather greeted the old woman with a hug. She

breathed in the aromas of the different pots and pans on the cooking range. She promised they would stay for lunch. The cook spooned some warm pudding into a bowl and made them taste it. It was buttery and gooey, loaded with plenty of plump black raisins. Jenny wondered if the old cook would share her recipe.

Cook's expression changed once Heather had eaten a few spoonfuls of pudding.

"Are you here for Brandon? That poor boy! Maybe you can coax him to eat a bite."

"I do want to talk to Brandon," Heather nodded, sharing a glance with Jenny. "But we were hoping to talk to you first."

The cook narrowed her eyes and trained them on Jenny.

"Girl, you playing Nancy Drew again?"

"Mrs. Newbury needs my help. I am going to try and find out what happened to Kelly."

"She didn't deserve to die," Cook said, wiping her eyes on her apron. "She was so sweet. She made Brandon happy."

"Can we talk to you about that night?" Heather asked.

"I was off duty that night," the old woman said. "Your

friend here took care of all the food."

"But you were helping serve the food, weren't you? I think I remember seeing you out in the courtyard."

"That's right."

"When did you last see Kelly?"

The cook's face clouded over. "I don't exactly remember. I brought her some of my leftover pot roast from the kitchen. She said she loved the spread you had put out but she was hankering for some of that roast from lunch."

Jenny figured Kelly was just buttering up the old cook. She had no idea why the young girl would do that. Either she was really good at heart or she had an ulterior motive. Or maybe she really liked pot roast. Although Kelly had been fawning over Jenny's food, she hadn't really seemed like a gourmand.

"What time was that?" she asked.

"Around nine," the cook answered. "That was before she had that fight with the missus."

"Do you know what that was about?" Heather asked curiously.

The cook was an old employee and apparently didn't think twice before speaking her mind.

"That woman doesn't need a reason to talk someone down. You know that!"

"Did Kelly stick around after her altercation with Ada?" Jenny asked.

"She seemed fine after that," Cook said, her admiration for the girl clear in her tone. "I don't know how much longer she stuck around though. I went to my quarters after ten. The party was still going strong at that time."

Jenny needed to establish what Kelly had been up to between the hours of ten and midnight.

"What about Megan? You know who Megan is, don't you?"

The cook frowned.

"That girl is trouble. She means no good, I can tell you that."

"How so?" Jenny asked.

"She's got her eye on Brandon. She was fixing to break those two up."

"Did Megan and Kelly talk to each other?"

The old woman bobbed her head up and down.

"Yes Sir! They said they were like sisters. You know that Megan's a smooth talker. She had Kelly believing whatever spurted out of her mouth."

"Was Megan here when you left?" Jenny asked the cook.

The woman didn't remember that.

"We were hoping to talk to some of the other people who were working that night."

A couple of girls came into the kitchen just then. They were both wearing staff uniforms.

"You can talk to them," Cook warned Heather. "But don't take too long. I have to start serving lunch soon."

She looked at the girls who were standing at a counter, stacking dishes.

"This lady wants to talk to you about the night of the party," Cook said, nodding toward Jenny. "There is no need to be afraid. Just tell her what you saw or heard."

Jenny introduced herself. They already knew who Heather was.

The girls had seen Ada argue with Kelly. They had also noticed how friendly Megan and Kelly had seemed to be.

"How long were you working that night?" Jenny asked them.

"We were here until the food ran out," one girl answered. "Most of the guests had left by that time."

"When was that?" Heather asked immediately.

"Sometime after 11," the other girl said. "I wasn't wearing my watch but I heard the big clock inside the house chime."

"Can you tell me who was still hanging around?"

One of the girls shook her head. The other hesitated.

"It's hard to say," she finally said. "Brandon was in and out of the house. Megan had left earlier but then she came back."

"What was Kelly doing?"

"Kelly was drunk," the first girl said and giggled.

"She wasn't that drunk," the other girl objected.

"So Brandon, Megan and Kelly were still at the party after 11," Jenny asked again.

She thought this timeline was important so she wanted to be sure of the facts.

A gong sounded somewhere in the distance.

"Time to start serving lunch," Cook said, suddenly snapping to attention.

She clapped her hands, bursting into a flurry of activity as she began plating the food. She pointed at the girls and started barking orders.

"You take the potatoes and green beans, and you, take the apple sauce and the rolls. I will bring out the chicken."

She looked at Heather and Jenny apologetically.

"Don't you go anywhere without tasting my food."

Jenny thanked the cook and reluctantly stepped out of the kitchen.

"What next?" she asked Heather.

"Let's go find Brandon."

Heather peeped into the dining room to make sure Brandon wasn't at the table. She took Jenny's hand and led her to a different part of the house.

Heather banged on the door insistently when her gentle knocks didn't produce an answer. The door finally burst open and Brandon stared out at them, bleary eyed. Jenny could barely recognize him.

"We need to talk," Heather said, rushing into the

room. "What's that smell?"

Jenny realized Brandon was still dressed in the same clothes he had been wearing at the party. Heather marched him into an ensuite bathroom. He reappeared a few minutes later, his face freshly scrubbed and his wet hair finger combed. Heather had dug out a fresh shirt for him.

"I'm sorry for your loss," Jenny said softly.

"I should never have come here," Brandon said bitterly. "We should have eloped, had a wedding in Vegas or something."

"You can't change what happened, B," Heather consoled him. "We have to move on. Jenny here is going to help find out who hurt Kelly."

"That won't bring her back."

"You're right," Heather agreed. "But it might keep your grandma from being arrested for a murder she didn't commit."

"Grandma never liked her," Brandon told them. "Apparently, Kelly wasn't good enough to be a Newbury."

"Do you think she was capable of harming her?" Jenny asked.

"Of course not!" Brandon said indignantly. "What kind of question is that?"

"Are you willing to talk to me?" Jenny asked him. "We need to figure out what happened that night."

Brandon sat down at the edge of the bed and waved his hand toward a couch set against the wall. Jenny accepted the silent invitation and sat down.

"What do you want to know?" Brandon asked, rubbing his eyes.

"When was the last time you ate something?" Heather demanded, noting the circles under Brandon's eyes.

He gave her a vague look. Heather stood up to leave.

"You can call the kitchen from here," Brandon said weakly. "But I'm not really hungry. I just want Kelly back."

Heather picked up the phone and pressed the code for the kitchen. She asked them to send food and coffee to the room.

"Where did you meet Kelly?" Jenny asked Brandon, hoping to ease into the conversation.

"At a party ... we hit it off."

"So it was love at first sight?" Jenny smiled.

"I was smitten," Brandon nodded. "I asked her out right away."

"Were you seeing Megan at that time?"

Brandon gave a snort.

"Megan had dumped me weeks ago. I had been mooning over her. But I forgot all about Megan when I went out with Kelly."

"When did you see her last on the night of the party?"

"Around 11 PM?" Brandon wasn't sure.

There was a knock on the door. A maid appeared with a tray of food. Heather forced Brandon to eat while Jenny took him through her set of questions. Nothing new came out of it. Brandon and Kelly had met Megan in the city. The girls seemed to get along well. Brandon hadn't realized he had spent more time with Megan at the party than he had with Kelly. According to him, he was just being a good host.

Jenny and Heather made a detour to the kitchen before they left. The fried chicken was pronounced perfect and Jenny begged the cook for the recipe.

"He's devastated," Heather remarked as Jenny drove back down the hill into town.

"What happened to Brandon's guests?" Jenny asked.

"Are they still in town?"

Heather had the contact information for a couple of Brandon's friends. She had met them at the party. She pulled out her phone and forwarded the info to Jenny.

"Are you going to call them now?" Heather asked.

"No time like the present," Jenny said, pulling up in front of the café.

Jenny went in and called Brandon's friends, armed with her usual questions.

"Brandon may be grieving now," one of them said. "But all was not well. There was trouble in paradise."

"Oh?"

Jenny crossed her fingers, wondering what the man on the phone was about to reveal.

"Kelly was having an affair. At least Brandon thought she was."

# Chapter 7

Jenny shared what she had learned from Brandon's friends with Heather the next morning. The two friends talked as they worked in the kitchen at the Boardwalk Café.

Jenny browned onions in a pot. She was trying out a new recipe for shrimp curry. Locals and tourists loved her food and she kept them happy by coming up with monthly specials. She had regularly cooked curry when she lived in the city and had once attended a class where they taught how to make authentic Indian curry. Over the years, Jenny had broken down the recipe into something simple that used regular grocery store ingredients.

"Do you believe this guy?" Heather asked her.

Heather was peeling garlic, a task she didn't relish at all.

"Hard to say," Jenny said, scraping the brown bits at the bottom of the pan where the onion was beginning to stick. "But there's no smoke without fire."

"Was he just being nasty?"

"Kelly's gone," Jenny reasoned. "Why would this guy want to smear her name?"

"Maybe she snubbed him," Heather shrugged. "Or, he's just stirring up trouble, having a laugh."

"That sounds mean."

"Yeah, but people do that, Jenny."

When Brandon's friend talked about Kelly having an affair, Jenny hadn't known what to think. He hadn't volunteered many details, just that Brandon suspected Kelly. Had Brandon intended to go ahead with the wedding? Or was he just biding time, trying to find out what Kelly was up to. Jenny reluctantly admitted that this gave Brandon a motive. Had he and Kelly had a fight about it? A fight that ended in Kelly landing in the pool?

"We need to go check out that pool," Jenny said to Heather. "Do you know where it is?"

"It's about fifty yards from that courtyard where we had the party. I used to go there a lot when I was a child."

"How does one get there?"

"It's on Ada's property, Jenny. You have to go through their front gate."

Ada Newbury had extended an open invite to Jenny. This kind of generosity was unheard of from Ada. Jenny assumed she had made an exception since her neck was on the line.

Jenny called ahead to let Ada know about her visit. Ada had to go out somewhere but she assured Jenny the security would let her in.

"How much more garlic do you need?" Heather grumbled.

Jenny looked at the small pile before Heather.

"That's enough. You can start peeling the ginger now."

Heather groaned and muttered through the process. The Magnolias arrived for lunch. They were the first group Jenny wanted to try out her recipe on. Star and Molly pronounced it delicious. Betty Sue declared it was too spicy.

Heather took a photo of the dish and posted it on social media.

Jenny and Heather set off after lunch. They breezed through the security gate and parked in front of the house.

Heather pointed to a paved path that wound through a clump of bushes.

"We can directly walk down to the pool. Do you want to do that?"

Jenny nodded her assent and set off at a brisk pace. The path took them around the house and beyond the courtyard. A couple of minutes later, Jenny turned a corner and stopped in her tracks.

A good sized building stood before her. A large pool with shimmering blue water lay inside a fancy enclosure. Plush cabanas with lime green cushions lined the pool on one side. Patio furniture with cozy sitting areas was arranged on the far side. There was a solid structure that looked like a pool house. It had a covered porch with a granite topped bar running along one wall. Jenny spotted another smaller pool in the distance. She guessed it was a hot tub.

"This is the pool complex," Heather said. "It used to be just the pool when I was younger. Ada turned it into this fancy thing a few years ago."

"How do we get in?" Jenny asked.

"I guess we open that door?" Heather pointed.

The door they spotted turned out to be locked. Jenny spotted a tiny button on one side. She pressed it, wondering if it was a doorbell of sorts. Her guess turned out to be right.

A tall, black haired youth with mussed hair ambled out on the covered porch. He wore a pair of sweat pants and nothing else. Heather and Jenny couldn't help but stare at his washboard stomach and six pack abs. Jenny recognized him as the guy who had found Kelly.

He gave them a wide smile and pressed some switch on the wall. The door slid open. The young man beckoned them over.

"Hello ladies," he beamed. "I'm Enrique. I take care of the pool."

Heather introduced them.

"Do you live here?" Jenny asked curiously.

"At the moment, yes," Enrique nodded. "Why don't you come in?"

Enrique opened a refrigerator and pulled out a few cans of soda. He offered them to the girls.

"I'm sure the boss won't mind," he grinned.

Jenny flipped the top off a can of ginger ale and took a big gulp. She was thinking about the locked door they had come through.

"Do people always ring that bell when they want to come in?" she asked.

Enrique shook his head.

"There's a digital access code. You have to enter it in a panel that's mounted by the side of the door."

"And how many people have that code?"

"Just the family, mostly. The boss is pretty stingy about handing it out. She doesn't like the staff using the pool."

"Isn't the pool already on private property?" Heather spoke her mind. "What's the need for all this security?"

Enrique shrugged.

"Like I said, the boss doesn't like anyone else using it. The maids used to take a dip all the time when they didn't have this whole enclosure. The missus didn't like that."

Jenny leaned forward and spoke softly.

"I'm sure they all know the code, eh?"

Enrique laughed readily.

"It's hard to keep it a secret," he nodded. "That's why they change it every week."

"That's too much!" Heather exclaimed.

"The boss gets what she wants," Enrique noted.

Jenny asked the question that had been rolling around in her mind.

"Did Kelly have the code?"

"I don't know," Enrique said. "Kelly was staying at the country club. There was no reason for her to have the code, unless someone gave it to her."

Jenny looked at Heather.

"So Kelly either had to have the code or someone let her in."

They both turned their heads around and stared at Enrique.

"Don't look at me," he said. "I didn't do it."

"Where were you the night of the party?"

"Right here," Enrique said. "Sleeping in my bed."

"You didn't see Kelly come in?"

"I didn't see or hear anyone," Enrique said. He looked sheepish. "I sneaked into the party and stole a couple of drinks from the bar." He looked down at the floor and muttered something. "Okay, I grabbed half a bottle of tequila. I was pretty drunk."

"You do realize there was a murder here that night?" Heather burst out. "How could you sleep through it?"

Enrique stretched his arms above his head and yawned.

"I didn't know there was going to be a murder here. I would have stayed awake if I knew."

Jenny realized Enrique was a smooth talker.

"Did you know Kelly?" Jenny asked.

She didn't get a straight answer.

"I saw her around here a couple of times," Enrique said.

"Did anyone else come to the pool that night?" she asked.

"I told you, I was fast asleep."

"What happens when someone enters the access code to get in?" Jenny asked. "Do you get some kind of indication inside?"

"I hear a beep," Enrique told them. "If it's during my working hours, I come out here."

It turned out that Enrique also acted as a lifeguard during the day. It was his job to keep an eye on whoever was using the pool and be ready to offer assistance.

"Are you allowed to have visitors?" Jenny asked.

"No visitors!" Enrique shook his head. "The boss will

fire my ass if I bring a girl here. And I'm not allowed to mingle with the maids either."

"That's a tough deal," Heather sympathized.

Enrique shrugged.

"It could be worse. I'm not complaining."

Jenny decided she wasn't going to get any more information out of Enrique. She wanted to take a stab at talking to Brandon again.

She walked back to the main house with Heather. Heather walked across the patio and opened a screen door.

"Ada doesn't like this," she giggled. "But she's not home."

A maid saw them and came over.

"Madam has asked you to go into the parlor."

It turned out Ada Newbury was home after all. She was wearing a snazzy outfit Jenny recognized as the latest in women's golf apparel.

"I just got back from my golf lesson. We were having tea."

Jenny looked around and realized there was someone

else in the room. A deeply tanned man with a mane of light brown hair sat in a wing chair near the fireplace. His long legs were stretched out before him and his tawny eyes were busy giving Jenny a once over.

"This is Zac," Ada said. "He's my golf coach."

Her cheeks turned pink while she introduced the man.

"Zac Gordon," the man drawled. "Like Ada said. I'm the golf pro over at the country club."

"I love golf," Jenny volunteered. "I'm a bit rusty, though. Haven't played a round in a while."

Zac sat up a bit.

"Come see me at the club. I'll fix you up right away."

"The country club is members only," Ada butted in. "It's not for everyone."

Zac winked at Jenny.

"Don't worry about that."

Ada clucked impatiently and motioned the girls toward a couch.

The girls took a seat. A couple of maids came in with tea and snacks. Jenny wasn't keen on talking about anything related to Kelly in the man's presence. Ada forced her hand.

"Did you have any more questions for me?"

"I wanted to take a look at the pool," Jenny explained. "I didn't realize it was a restricted area."

Ada waited until the maids left the room.

"The staff takes undue advantage. They took midnight dips in the pool. Some of the girls even brought men over. I had to get that enclosure built."

"We met Enrique," Heather supplied. "He told us about the access codes."

"How many people know those codes, Mrs. Newbury?" Jenny asked.

"Just the family," Ada said. "I make sure of that."

"How do you think Kelly got in there? Did Brandon give her the code?"

Ada turned red.

"He shouldn't have. Kelly wasn't family."

"What are you saying?" Heather burst out. "Brandon was going to marry her in just a few days."

"He wouldn't have gone ahead with the wedding," Ada said suddenly.

Jenny didn't know whether to believe Ada. Was it just wishful thinking on her part? Did she have a concrete plan to split up the couple? Why was she so confident of getting Kelly out of the way?

"Brandon's broken up over Kelly," Heather observed. "I think he loved her a lot."

Jenny steered the question back to the access codes.

"The important thing here is how Kelly got into the pool house."

Zac Gordon spoke up, shocking Jenny with his assertion.

"That pool boy let her in, of course."

"Enrique? Why do you think that?"

"They were having an affair," Zac said with relish. "Kelly was two timing Brandon, seeing the pool boy on the side."

Ada didn't look surprised.

"Did you know about this?" Heather asked her.

Ada's mouth twisted in disgust.

"That girl was not right for my Brandon."

Zac Gordon was looking pleased with himself. Jenny

asked the question uppermost in her mind.

"Wait a minute, Zac. How did you know Kelly?"

# Chapter 8

Adam and Jenny were having dinner at Seaview, the three storied ocean facing house Jenny now called home. Adam brought a bottle of the local wine Jenny liked. They started their meal with crab cakes and caught up on what Jenny had been up to.

Jenny told Adam about meeting Enrique.

"Who is this Enrique?" Adam asked, simmering with anger. "He didn't come forward when we interviewed all the staff."

"He wasn't working at the party," Jenny explained. "Maybe that's why his name never came up."

"I'm going to talk to him first thing tomorrow."

"He looks like a player," Jenny said with a smile.

She wanted to talk to Enrique herself.

The next morning, Jenny arrived at the café at 5 AM and started prepping for the day. Star came in around eight and helped Jenny serve breakfast. The Magnolias came in after the crowd thinned.

"Ready to hit the road?" Heather asked Jenny.

"I'm ready," Jenny nodded.

The girls were going back to talk to Enrique.

Jenny hated to impose on Star all the time. She promised to be back in an hour and set off with Heather.

The girls took the path that led to the pool house. They rang the bell again, waiting for Enrique. There was a click as the door unlocked. Jenny took it as an invitation to enter and went in. She walked around the pool and went to the covered porch, calling out for Enrique. He didn't look too happy when he came out. Jenny was relieved to see he was fully dressed this time.

"I didn't know you had a uniform?" Heather remarked. "It suits you."

"Everyone working on the estate has to wear one," Enrique said with a shrug. "Are you here for a dip in the pool?"

"Can we do that?" Heather asked, surprised.

"I don't see why not," Enrique said. "You are on the list."

"What list?" Jenny asked.

"The list of people who can come in here," Enrique said in a bored voice. "Looks like this lady here is some relation of the Newburys."

Heather actually was a Newbury, although she didn't use that name.

"Grandpa must have added my name," Heather surmised. "I haven't been here in ages though."

Jenny gazed at Enrique.

"Did you talk to the police?"

"They were just here," Enrique grumbled. "Grilled me for an hour. I told them the same thing I told you. I slept right through that party."

"You're sure you didn't let Kelly in?"

"100%."

"How well did you know Kelly?"

"I met her when she came to the pool once or twice with Brandon. She was the friendly kind. Not stuck up like some of the boss's guests."

"You hit it off, huh?" Jenny asked.

Enrique took a deep breath.

"What are you suggesting?"

"Were you having an affair with Kelly?"

Enrique threw back his head and laughed.

"You can't be serious."

"Just answer me, Enrique," Jenny said, refusing to back down. "Were you and Kelly having an affair?"

"Of course not!" Enrique said irritably. "What gave you that idea?"

"I heard you were," Jenny persisted. "Why would someone say that?"

"I don't know … to get me in trouble?"

"Come on," Jenny cajoled. "You can talk to me. I know how pretty Kelly was. I know how a young buck like you would be attracted to her."

Enrique looked over his shoulder.

"Kelly wasn't just pretty, okay? She was friendly too. She didn't mind chatting with the help."

"So you flirted with her a bit?" Jenny smiled.

She wanted Enrique to get comfortable with her.

"It was the other way around," Enrique said. "Kelly came on to me. I had to push her away a couple of times."

Jenny didn't have trouble imagining that. Enrique was

the male version of a hot swimsuit model.

"You didn't find her attractive?"

Enrique gave his usual shrug.

"I'm not blind, lady. But she was the boss's girl. I would be out on my hide if I so much as looked at her."

Jenny decided to give him the benefit of the doubt.

"She must have felt snubbed."

"She backed off. I didn't think too much about it."

Enrique sounded sincere. Jenny wondered if Adam had been able to get more out of him.

The girls went back to the Boardwalk Café.

Jenny made a batch of shrimp curry for lunch. She had tweaked the recipe after taking feedback from the Magnolias.

Adam came to the café for lunch.

"I hear you visited the pool boy?" Jenny asked as she placed a platter of rice and curry on the table.

Adam pursed his lips.

"Nothing ever stays secret in this town."

Jenny laughed as she spooned some curry on Adam's plate.

"There is no gossip involved this time. I have it from the horse's mouth."

"You met Enrique again?" Adam asked, leaning forward.

Jenny told him about her latest trip to the Newbury place.

"I hope you were not alone."

"Heather went with me," Jenny said. "But that's beside the point. Why can't I go alone? I can take care of myself."

"Will you listen to me this time?"

"Don't be so controlling, Adam. Enrique is just a harmless boy. He's the same age as Nicky."

Adam ate a bite and sat back. He complimented the food.

"I ran a background check," he said reluctantly. "That harmless boy as you call him was almost convicted."

Jenny sat down with a thump.

"What did he do?"

"He molested a girl," Adam said bluntly. "At least, that's what he was arrested for. But the charges didn't stick."

"Do you know why?"

"The girl refused to testify. Rumor is he threatened her."

"Wow!" Jenny exclaimed. "Was it a local girl?"

"She was local alright. She was a year younger than him. They dated for a while."

"They dated?" Jenny was curious. "Could it have been a lovers' tiff?"

She grudgingly admitted to herself that Enrique must have charmed her. She found it hard to believe he was capable of doing anything wrong.

Adam slapped a hand on the table.

"That's exactly what the girl said later. She said they had a falling out and she wanted to get back at him. But she later realized it wasn't the right thing to do. So she dropped the charges and Enrique got away."

"Or he was really innocent," Jenny said stoutly.

"All I'm saying is, be careful around this guy."

"Fine," Jenny said. "I'll keep that in mind. Now tell me how you like the curry."

Adam had cleared his plate while they were talking. He asked for seconds.

"You have another winner, Jenny. This shrimp curry is perfect. It's spicy and exotic but so familiar."

"Is it too exotic for Pelican Cove?"

"Give us some credit," Adam said. "I know we like our down home favorites but we do appreciate variety. And the tourists are going to love it too."

Jenny was pleased. She served herself some of the curry and dug in.

"Who's your top suspect?" she asked Adam after a while. "Is Ada off your list now?"

"You know I can't discuss that with you, Jenny," Adam sighed.

"It all depends on the motive, doesn't it?" Jenny continued. "What did anyone gain by killing a sweet young girl like Kelly?"

"Money?" Adam said reluctantly.

"I don't think so," Jenny said. "Kelly was an orphan and she had a regular office job. She was definitely marrying up. I don't think she had a dime to spare for anyone."

"We didn't find much in her room, other than a few clothes and make-up. No jewelry."

"What about a phone?" Jenny asked suddenly. "She must have had a cell phone. Everyone has one."

"She did have a phone," Adam nodded. "The techs are looking at it."

"Did you go through the phone?" Jenny asked.

"Not yet. Why?"

"That phone could have a lot of answers. Can I have a look at it please?"

"Nice try!" Adam snorted. "That phone is part of the evidence. You won't get anywhere near it."

"Did you find it near the pool?" Jenny asked.

Adam didn't reply.

"If you didn't find it near the pool, it's not really part of the crime scene, is it?"

"It's part of Kelly's personal effects at the very least," Adam said.

"Who gets access to that stuff?"

"Her family, I guess," Adam said.

"She doesn't have any," Jenny reminded him. "Brandon might be her next of kin since he was her fiancé. What if Brandon puts in a request for that phone?"

"Okay, stop," Adam said, holding both his hands up. "What do you want?"

"I just want to look at the phone for a few minutes," Jenny said with a smile. "I won't take it out of your sight. In fact, we can look at it together."

"What do you hope to achieve by this?"

"I won't know until I look."

Adam arranged to meet Jenny in a couple of hours. Jenny served the last customers of the day and closed the café. She walked to the police station, feeling excited. She had a strong intuition that Kelly's phone would point them in the right direction.

Adam sat in his office, staring at a phone encased in a plastic bag. He told Jenny to sit down.

"I'm as curious as you are," he said. "Let's get this show on the road."

He pulled on a pair of gloves and picked up the phone. The battery had discharged. Adam pulled a charger from a drawer and plugged the phone in. The voice mail icon came on.

"Looks like she has a lot of messages."

Jenny had walked around the desk to stand behind Adam. She peered at the phone over his shoulder. She asked him to press a bunch of keys and read off the screen.

"Who's Paula?" she asked Adam. "Have you come across anyone by that name?"

Adam declined.

"Looks like Kelly was quite friendly with this person. She's called her multiple times a day and messaged her several times in an hour."

Kelly had called Brandon too. Adam pointed it out.

"Of course she called Brandon. They were engaged, weren't they? And look, there's a call to Megan."

"So what does this prove?" Adam frowned. "Kelly liked calling people?"

"That's what kids do these days," Jenny reminded him. "Remember Nick and the twins?"

She was referring to her son and Adam's twin girls. They had met in Pelican Cove and established a rapport almost instantly. They texted each other several times a day. Jenny complained Nick called the twins more often than he called her.

"What are you saying?"

"This generation needs to share everything. They text their friends every time they sneeze or poop. Kelly was doing the same."

"I still don't get it," Adam said.

"Whoever this Paula is, she meant a lot to Kelly. She must have been her go-to friend. The one person Kelly wanted to tell everything."

"We need to find out who Paula is," Adam said, catching on.

"That's right," Jenny said.

"I don't think there was anyone by this name at the party," Adam said, going through a list on his desk.

"You're right," Jenny agreed. "I don't remember meeting anyone by this name either."

"If this Paula was such a good friend," Adam mused, "why wasn't she at the party?"

"Maybe Paula is code for something else," Jenny said. "Or someone else."

"That sounds farfetched," Adam said.

"Not really," Jenny said, reluctant to give up on her theory. "It could be a nickname."

"So how do you propose to find this Paula?" Adam asked.

Jenny pulled up Paula's number in Kelly's address book and pressed the call button. The call went to voicemail.

"Looks like this phone is switched off."

"What now?" Adam asked.

"I'm going to talk to Brandon. If Kelly was so close to this Paula, Brandon must surely know her."

# Chapter 9

The spring sun bathed Pelican Cove in bright light. A cool ocean breeze made people keep their sweaters on. The sunlight wasn't strong enough to warm the skin. The Magnolias braved the weather and sat out on the deck at the Boardwalk Café.

Betty Sue carried on with her knitting, pausing only to take a sip of her coffee. Jenny brought out a tray loaded with tiny parfaits.

"I took your advice," she told her aunt. "These parfaits have layers of shaved chocolate. Why don't you try one and let me know if it tastes good?"

Heather walked up the boardwalk, tugging her black poodle Tootsie along with her. She tied Tootsie to a post and bounded up the stairs.

"I'll have one of those," she said, picking up a parfait cup.

"How's your investigation coming along?" Betty Sue asked Jenny.

"That's a big word," Jenny winced. "I'm just trying to figure out what happened."

"Did you try calling that number again?" Heather

asked, referring to the number Jenny had found in Kelly's phone.

"The phone's still switched off," Jenny said. "It's highly suspicious."

Betty Sue and Star wanted to know what the girls were talking about. Jenny explained how Kelly had frequently been in touch with a girl called Paula.

"I think it belongs to a man," Betty Sue said.

"Why do you say that?" Jenny asked, surprised.

"It's a code, girl. We used to do that all the time."

"Huh?" Heather sat up. "You had a cell phone?"

Betty Sue rolled her eyes.

"Don't be ridiculous, Heather!"

She took a deep breath and stared at the ocean. Her voice turned softer.

"I was young once. There was this boy my Daddy didn't like. We, my friend Lily and I, gave him a name. We called him Ruth. We used to talk about him all the time and no one was the wiser. My Daddy thought Ruth was a girl who lived on the other side of town."

"Betty Sue! You sneaky devil!" Star laughed.

"So you think Paula is a guy?" Jenny asked Betty Sue.

"I don't agree," Heather said. "Times have changed, Grandma. It's perfectly okay to be friends with a guy. It's not taboo anymore."

"And Kelly wasn't a teen staying at home with her parents," Jenny reasoned. "She was an independent woman who lived alone. She could talk to anyone she wanted to, guy or girl."

"Cheating on your beau is still frowned upon though, right?" Betty Sue asked.

"You didn't spend much time with Kelly," Heather told Betty Sue. "She was very friendly. She must have been like that with everyone."

Jenny was lost in thought. She was thinking about the repercussions of Kelly having an affair.

"Remember what Brandon's friend said?" she spoke up. "What if Kelly was seeing someone behind Brandon's back? He wouldn't like that."

"You think Brandon knew?" Heather asked. "Why was he going ahead with the wedding, then?"

"I can't answer that," Jenny said. "We need to talk to Brandon."

Was Brandon the vindictive kind, Jenny wondered. What if he had caught Kelly with another man? Would he harm Kelly in a fit of anger?

Heather and Jenny set off for the Newbury estate after lunch. Brandon was sitting out in the courtyard, staring in the distance. Jenny sat before him and waited for him to speak.

Brandon sighed heavily after a few minutes.

"I miss her. What am I going to do without her, Heather?"

Heather patted his hand but said nothing.

"What time did you turn in on the night of the party?" Jenny asked.

"10, 10:30?" Brandon looked at her blankly. "I don't remember."

"When was the last time you talked to Kelly?"

"We barely talked during the party," Brandon said bitterly. "Megan was here and we were catching up with old friends. Kelly was hanging out with Binkie."

"That was kind of odd," Jenny observed. "Many people thought you and Megan were the happy couple."

"What people?" Brandon asked, sounding angry.

"I could use a drink," Jenny said, getting up. "Do you want something?"

"I can ring for sweet tea," Brandon said.

"It's okay," Jenny told him. "I'm going inside anyway. I'll let the kitchen staff know."

She went into the house, leaving Heather with Brandon. The house was quiet inside. Jenny wondered where Ada was. She pushed open the kitchen door. The old cook sat at a small table with her feet up on a chair. She looked sleepy.

"Hello," Jenny greeted her. "I'm Heather's friend. I was here a couple of days ago …"

"I know who you are, missy," the cook interrupted her. "How can I help you?"

"I'm trying to determine everyone's whereabouts the night of the party," Jenny explained. "How long was the staff around, do you know?"

"Most guests left by ten," the cook said. "Some of the young ones still hung around, I'm sure."

The door opened and a maid came in. Jenny remembered she had been serving food at the party. She repeated her question.

"I was around for a while after ten," the maid said evasively.

"This is between us," Jenny assured her. "I am not going to report you to Mrs. Newbury."

The maid hesitated.

"The missus went in around 9:30. The courtyard was empty by 11."

"How long did you stick around?" Jenny asked.

"My boyfriend came over," the girl said reluctantly. "I picked up a bottle of wine from the bar and we sat out in the garden, drinking."

"Did you see anyone walking toward the pool?" Jenny asked eagerly.

"We weren't really paying attention," the girl said. "If you know what I mean …"

Jenny knew what she meant.

"You didn't see a single person out in the courtyard after 11?"

"I didn't say that," the maid said. "Brandon came out around 11:30. I saw him from the corner of my eye."

"Do you think he saw you?"

The girl shrugged.

"We were standing in a dark corner, so maybe not."

"Where did he go?"

"I don't know," the girl said. "He was there one minute, then he was gone."

"But you're sure you saw him?"

The girl nodded emphatically.

Jenny spoke to the cook.

"Can we have some sweet tea, please?"

"Sure," the cook drawled. "I'll send someone out there, don't worry."

Jenny walked back to the courtyard. Brandon had a frown on his face as Heather chatted with him.

"I'm parched," he said, looking up at Jenny. "What's taking them so long?"

"You told me you turned in around ten the night of the party," Jenny said, taking a seat.

"And?"

"It looks like you came out of your room around 11:30. You were seen walking around here."

Brandon was looking bewildered.

"What were you doing out here, Brandon?" Jenny asked. "Were you looking for Kelly?"

"I don't know what you are talking about."

"Did you know Kelly was going to be at the pool? Did you arrange to meet her there? Maybe the two of you wanted to take a midnight dip."

"Kelly wasn't staying here," Brandon said, rubbing his forehead. "She had a room at the country club."

"You could still have met her at the pool house," Jenny pressed.

"But I didn't," Brandon said.

"What were you doing out here so late at night?"

"I don't know," Brandon pleaded. "I honestly don't know. I must have been walking in my sleep."

"That's convenient," Jenny muttered.

"Since when do you sleep walk?" Heather asked.

"It started a few months ago," Brandon told her. "I do it when I am stressed about something."

"What did you have to stress about?" Heather scoffed. "You were marrying the love of your life."

"I don't know, Heather," Brandon whined. "I don't control it."

Jenny didn't believe the sleepwalking theory. She was sure Brandon had just made it up on the spot.

"Were you following Kelly?" she asked softly, leaning toward Brandon.

"Why would I do that?" Brandon cried.

"Look, we think Kelly might have been having an affair. Did you know about it?"

"Kelly would never cheat on me," Brandon protested. "She was a good kid."

Jenny looked at Brandon, trying to read his mind. She didn't believe he was that ignorant.

"Kelly sent a lot of messages to someone," Jenny told Brandon. "Did you notice she was using her phone a lot?"

Brandon seemed to hesitate a bit. Then his face crumpled.

"You're right. Kelly might have been having an affair."

"What made you suspect her?"

"It's like you said," Brandon explained. "She was on

the phone a lot, even when she was with me. I even joked about it. She said it was a friend who was in distress. She needed to hold her hand."

"That's possible," Jenny nodded, considering what Brandon said. "But not probable. If she was so close to this friend, why didn't she introduce you to her?"

"That's what I thought too," Brandon said bitterly.

"If you suspected Kelly, why were you going ahead with the wedding?" Heather asked.

"I was hopeful," Brandon said. "I thought maybe she was having a last fling."

"You're saying you would have been fine with that?" Jenny asked incredulously.

Brandon clutched his head and groaned.

"I have a headache. Can we talk later?"

He stood up and started walking inside.

Jenny and Heather talked about what had happened on the way back.

"I'm sure he's lying," Jenny declared. "He's hiding something."

"I believe Brandon," Heather said supportively. "He

was hopeful in spite of his suspicions. That's a man in love."

Jenny dropped Heather off at the Bayview Inn and stopped at Mama Rosa's, the island's pizzeria, on the way home. She was feeling exhausted and was in no mood to cook dinner. She ran into Jason.

"Hey Jenny!" he greeted her.

They chatted while their order was getting ready.

"Are you eating pizza every night?" Jenny admonished. "Why don't you cook something simple at home?"

"Cooking for one is a chore," Jason said. "Most days, I'm too tired anyway."

Jenny extended a dinner invitation and made Jason order a salad with his pizza.

That night, Jenny thought about Jason as she walked on the beach. Jason had been recovering from a bad breakup for the past year. She wanted him to be happy. Even though she had chosen Adam over Jason, she cared deeply for him. Deep down, she felt a bit guilty for turning him down.

Dark clouds lined the horizon when Jenny stepped out of her house the next morning. The sky was overcast and a chilly wind whipped Jenny's hair around. She headed to the Boardwalk Café and started getting breakfast ready.

Jenny pulled out a pan of freshly baked banana nut muffins just as the clock struck six. The phone rang before she had a chance to open the café doors. It was Jason.

Jenny rushed to Jason's house, praying that everything was alright. She had been unable to make sense of Jason's gibberish. He had been hysterical and Jenny had promised to go see him right away.

Jenny scrambled out of her car a few minutes later. Jason was standing out on the porch, white in the face. He held a pink colored bundle in his hands. He stood there dumbly, staring at Jenny.

"What's wrong, Jason?" Jenny cried. "What's going on?"

Jason held his arms out to Jenny.

"Emily," he mumbled.

"Speak up, Jason."

A wail arose from the bundle before Jason had a chance to say anything.

"This is Emily," he said, staring at the bundle in his hands. "Emily Stone."

Jenny's eyes widened as she realized what Jason held. She gently eased the bundle out of his arms and stared down at the chubby infant. A pair of brown, almond shaped eyes stared back at her. The baby gurgled and waved a fist in the air, demanding attention.

"Where did she come from?" Jenny asked softly, looking up at Jason.

# Chapter 10

Jenny bustled through the breakfast rush at the Boardwalk Café. After grabbing a cup of coffee and a muffin for herself, she made a batch of her banana caramel parfaits. Heather arrived right on time to taste them.

Heather dug into the delicious treat as Jenny dialed the number she had been calling for the last couple of days. She muttered an oath when the standard recording came on. The phone was still switched off.

"Any luck?" Heather asked with her mouth full.

"I'm beginning to think someone chucked this phone into the ocean."

"You may be right," Heather said seriously. "You need Adam's help here."

"I'm going to talk to him," Jenny said, her mouth set in a firm line. "Are you sticking around here?"

Heather nodded.

"Grandma will be here soon. You go ahead. I will keep an eye on things here."

Jenny walked the couple of blocks to the police station,

hoping Adam wasn't too busy. The front desk was deserted and Nora, the desk clerk, was nowhere in sight. Jenny knocked on Adam's door and went in.

Adam sat with his leg propped up on a chair.

"Is your leg bothering you again?" Jenny asked with concern.

"No more than usual," Adam said with a shrug. "What are you doing here, Jenny?"

"I tried that number again," Jenny said, pulling up a chair. "No response."

"You don't give up, do you?"

"You need to trace this number, Adam. Find out who it belongs to."

"Are you trying to tell me how to do my job?" Adam asked, suppressing a grin. "You know better than that, Jenny."

"All I'm saying is, this phone is important. It could be our biggest lead."

"Our?"

"Whatever," Jenny snapped. "This Paula person was close to Kelly. We need to hunt her down so we can talk to her."

"I agree with you this time," Adam said. "I'm already on it."

"Will you let me know when you learn something?" Jenny asked.

"I can't promise that," Adam said honestly. "It's all part of my investigation. I'm not obligated to share any information with you, Jenny. You on the other hand, are."

Jenny stood up in a huff and stalked out. Adam was very particular about keeping his professional life separate from his personal one. She just wished he would cut her some slack once in a while.

Jenny took the scenic route back to the café, going over everything she knew about Kelly so far. She spotted a few familiar faces on the beach and waved at them. A bright cornflower blue sky stretched above her with not a single cloud in sight. Many tourists seemed to have taken advantage of the fair weather and were beginning to arrive on the beach.

Jenny spotted the Magnolias sitting out on the deck of the Boardwalk Café and her face broke into a smile. She picked up her pace, eager to join the lively discussion that seemed to be on.

"What do you say, Jenny?" Betty Sue asked as soon as she spotted Jenny coming up the café's steps. "Can Jason take care of Emily?"

Jason Stone and his baby girl Emily had become the talk of the town. Jason had told Jenny the whole story after he had come out of his initial shock. There wasn't much to tell. His doorbell had rung early in the morning. He opened the door to find a baby on his doorstep. His baby.

There was a small note tucked in the baby's blanket. It was from Kandy, a city lawyer who had unceremoniously dumped Jason and disappeared from his life. As it turned out, Kandy had been pregnant. She decided she wanted to have the child on her own. A few months after Emily was born, Kandy had come to a new decision. There was no room for a baby in her life. She had left the baby on Jason's doorstep, probably believing he would take care of her.

Jason had come out of his daze after a day or two. He was overjoyed. In his late forties, Jason had given up all hope of ever becoming a father. Emily was a gift he cherished with all his heart. His aunt Linda had taken one look at the baby and declared she was 100% Stone. Jason had turned his home office into a nursery.

The old biddies in town wondered how a single man, a confirmed bachelor, could raise a child on his own. But Jenny believed in Jason.

"Of course he can," she said supportively. "He's going to be the best father you ever came across."

"But can he do it alone?" Molly asked. "You know what they say. It takes a village to raise a child."

"And we have that village here," Jenny said brightly. "I have signed up for babysitting duty. I can't wait to wrap that little munchkin in my arms."

"Jason's out of town a lot," Star reminded Jenny. "Who's going to take care of the baby then?"

"He can hire a full time nanny," Heather said.

"Or he can reduce his workload," Jenny said. "I'm sure Jason will figure it out."

"It's been a while since I bounced a baby on my knee," Betty Sue sighed. "I wouldn't mind looking after that little one sometime."

"I'm not changing any diapers," Heather groaned, wrinkling her nose. "But I can play with her."

"I can read her a story," Molly joined in.

The group broke up after a while and Jenny started making lunch. Two hours later, she collapsed into a chair in the kitchen, exhausted.

The café had been busy and they had sold out of everything.

"I saved a sandwich for you," her aunt said, pulling out

a plate covered in plastic wrap from the refrigerator. "There's half a cup of soup left."

Jenny took a big bite of the sandwich and warmed the soup in the microwave. Something had been niggling at the back of her mind all day. The fog in her mind cleared suddenly and she almost choked on her sandwich. Star patted her on the back as she started coughing.

"What's the matter, sweetie?"

"How could I forget that?" Jenny chided herself and cleared her throat.

"Why don't you finish eating first?" her aunt suggested calmly.

Jenny took a couple of minutes to finish chewing her sandwich.

"Ada had an argument with Kelly on the night of the party," she explained. "I was going to talk to Ada about it but I completely forgot."

"You can do it now," Star said.

"Do you want to go with me?" Jenny asked.

Ada Newbury was a snob. She only talked to a small bunch of people in town. Star wasn't one of them.

"I have no wish to be insulted by that monster," Star smirked. "You go ahead."

Heather was busy working at the inn so Jenny set off for the Newbury estate on her own. The security guards waved her through, and the maid who greeted her at the door led her into Ada's parlor.

Ada's mouth twisted in a grimace when she saw Jenny.

"Have you considered calling ahead?" she asked haughtily. "I'm afraid I have a golf lesson in fifteen minutes."

"We need to talk," Jenny said, ignoring Ada's thinly veiled rebuke.

"I'll be back in a couple of hours. You can wait here until then. But it might be better if you came back with an appointment."

Jenny sat down on a sofa and looked up at Ada.

"Do you want to find out what happened to Kelly?" she asked calmly. "I don't have to do this, Mrs. Newbury."

Ada rolled her eyes and sat down opposite Jenny.

"I suppose I can cancel my golf lesson."

She picked up a phone and dialed someone. She turned

her back on Jenny and talked softly into the phone. She hung up a couple of minutes later.

"I postponed my appointment," she explained. "I'm lucky my coach agreed to move some things around."

Jenny got to the point.

"People saw you arguing with Kelly on the night of the party. Can you tell me what that was about?"

"Just wedding stuff," Ada said.

"Can you be more specific?"

"Brandon doesn't know about this," Ada said softly, looking over her shoulder.

"I'll try to keep this to myself."

"That girl wasn't right," Ada complained, back in form. "I was giving her the wedding of a lifetime. A poor orphan like her, getting married at the country club? Any other girl would have been grateful."

"What did Kelly do?"

"She didn't want the club wedding. She was happy with a civil ceremony. She wanted me to take the money I would spend on the country club wedding and give it to her."

"But why?" Jenny asked, perplexed.

"She said she needed it for a down payment on a house, the house she and Brandon would live in after they got married."

"That's not a bad idea," Jenny shrugged.

"Brandon already has a place of his own," Ada dismissed. "There was no need to go buy another house."

"Didn't Kelly know that?"

"Of course she did," Ada cried. "I think she just wanted my money. She would have taken the money and run."

Jenny wondered if Kelly had been that calculating.

"Leaving Brandon at the altar?" Jenny asked.

"I wouldn't put it past her," Ada said strongly.

"I need to find out more about this argument," Jenny told Ada. "I'm going to talk to a few more people."

"Do that," Ada said curtly. "And call before coming next time."

Jenny wandered through the house, hoping to run into some of the staff that had been working the night of the party. She gravitated toward the kitchen. The cook greeted her like an old friend.

"Got more questions for me?" she asked.

"It's about the fight Ada had with Kelly. I want to find out more about it."

The cook picked up a wall mounted phone and pressed a button. She asked the person at the other end to come into the kitchen. Jenny guessed it was an internal line.

Jenny recognized the maid who walked into the kitchen a few minutes later.

"This is about the night of the party," Jenny began. "You saw Mrs. Newbury arguing with Kelly, right?"

"Those two were ready to gauge each other's eyes out," the girl said with a grin.

"Do you know what happened?"

"It was about money," the girl said, climbing up on a tall stool next to the big kitchen island. She picked up a carrot from a pile and started peeling it. "I think the boss wanted her to go away and leave Mr. Brandon alone."

Jenny could imagine Ada doing that.

"Are you sure about that?"

The girl became defensive.

"Kelly was saying she didn't care about the money. She just wanted to make Brandon happy."

"What else?"

The girl's voice dropped as she leaned toward Jenny.

"The boss got all red in the face. Told Kelly she better listen to her or else. Then she pushed Kelly."

"I can't imagine Ada doing that," Jenny said skeptically.

"Talk to the others," the girl said. "They will tell you the same thing."

Jenny spent the next hour talking to other members of Ada's domestic staff. All of them had watched the altercation between the two women. Each of them had their own theory about what the fight was about. They all seemed to agree on two things. Money had been mentioned. And Ada Newbury had pushed Kelly.

Jenny felt confused on the drive back home. She knew Ada was a snob and loved talking down to people she didn't consider her equals. Jenny could well imagine Ada looking down her nose at Kelly, calling her names. She could even imagine Ada offering the girl a bunch of money to leave Brandon alone. But was Ada Newbury capable of physically assaulting someone?

# Chapter 11

Jenny had a surprise waiting for her when she got home. Her son Nick sat dozing on the sofa, his feet up on the coffee table.

"Nicky!" Jenny cried joyfully. "When did you get here?"

She had no idea he had been planning a visit home.

Nick sat up and rubbed his eyes. His youthful face broke into a smile. He leapt up and wrapped Jenny in a tight hug.

"I missed you, Mom," he said. "I just wanted to spend some time with you. Is that okay?"

"Of course it's okay," Jenny said, planting a kiss on his cheek. "You don't need permission to come home."

"You sure I'm not upsetting any weekend plans?" Nick asked with a grin.

"Don't be silly," Jenny dismissed.

Nick was a junior in college. He wanted to be a lawyer like his father.

"Why didn't you warn me you were coming?" Jenny

asked as she walked into the kitchen. "I would have stocked up on your favorite stuff."

"I'm not here for the food, Mom," Nick grinned. "I mean, not just for the food," he said with a wink. "Whatever you cook is going to be great."

Jenny inspected the refrigerator, noting its meager contents.

"How about meatloaf for dinner?" she asked. "We will get fresh fish at the market tomorrow."

Star arrived and exclaimed over Nick.

Dinner was a lively meal, with Nick regaling them with anecdotes of his campus life.

Jenny and Nick sat out on the patio later, sipping coffee. The salty air was a bit chilly, but pleasant enough to sit outside. A large stone water fountain gurgled a few feet away and a gibbous moon rose in the sky.

"How's Adam?" Nick asked his mother. "Is he behaving himself?"

Jenny punched her son in the arm.

"Don't get fresh."

"Seriously, Mom," Nick said. "Is he treating you well?

I know he tends to fly off the handle sometimes."

"You don't have to worry about that," Jenny assured him. "Adam's changed a bit. For the better."

"I'm glad to hear that," Nick nodded, sounding decades older than twenty. "When are you getting married?"

Jenny blushed.

"We haven't set a date yet. What's the rush?"

"You know you have my blessing?" Nick asked her. "I'm with you whatever you decide to do. You can dump the guy or marry him tomorrow. It's your call."

"I'll keep that in mind," Jenny said lightly. "Now let's talk about your grades."

Nick groaned and launched into a lengthy explanation of why he had dropped one class and was barely scraping through in another.

Jenny woke before the sun rose the next morning. She had a big smile on her face as she got ready to go to the café. Having her son home really made her happy. She drove to the café as the sky lightened and an orange glow crept over the horizon.

Adam surprised her by coming to the café for breakfast. Jenny stood by his table as he tucked into his crab omelet.

"Have you found anything new?" she asked, topping up his coffee.

"I have," Adam nodded. "We got back Paula's phone records."

Jenny waited for Adam to go on. He ignored her and got back to eating his omelet.

"What do the records say?" Jenny asked, refusing to back down.

"They belong to someone called Paula Briggs, okay?" Adam said, sounding exasperated. "And the phone was in the vicinity of Kelly's phone."

"So whoever Paula is, she wasn't far away," Jenny summed up.

She thought over the different people she had met at Ada's, focusing on girls she had seen Kelly talking to. She immediately thought of Megan. Could Kelly have been talking to Megan?

Jenny didn't voice her suspicions to Adam. She was sure he would forbid her to do anything. She planned her next move and sat down to have a cup of coffee with Adam.

"Does Jason really have a kid?" Adam asked.

"He sure does. You have to meet Emily. She's the cutest baby you ever saw. We should all have dinner sometime."

Adam muttered something under his breath.

"Kind of weird, huh?" he said, looking dazed. "At his age."

"What's wrong with his age?" Jenny demanded. "Jason's going to make a great dad."

Adam finally left. Jenny rushed to the phone and called Heather.

"Can you come over?" she asked.

The two girls headed to Megan's. Jenny purposely didn't call ahead. She didn't want to give Megan any time to prepare herself.

Megan seemed a bit tired. She didn't look too happy to see them.

"You were around Kelly a lot, weren't you?" Jenny asked directly.

"We were both at the same party," Megan said. "Just like you."

"Were the two of you up to something?"

"We were planning to go shopping in the city," Megan said, looking bewildered. "Didn't we talk about this before?"

"What I mean is, were you hiding something from Brandon?"

"Why would I do that?" Megan asked wearily. "Brandon is my friend, not Kelly."

Heather tried to help Jenny.

"What she means is … maybe Kelly wanted to surprise Brandon or something. She could have asked for your help. You see what we are getting at?"

Megan shook her head.

"Kelly and I didn't talk about Brandon at all. We just discussed some girl stuff. Fashion, work stuff, life in the city …"

"So you two hit it off?" Jenny murmured.

Megan shrugged.

"I guess you could say that. I thought I made a new friend. It gets pretty lonely in the city, you know, living on your own. It's hard to find someone who understands what you are going through." Megan's voice sounded hoarse with emotion. "Doesn't matter now. Kelly's gone."

Jenny and Heather took their leave. Megan made it clear she was happy to see them go.

"What do you think?" Heather asked as soon as they got into the car. "Was she lying?"

Jenny said nothing for a while.

"Could Megan and Kelly have been plotting something together?"

"Like what?" Heather asked, raising her eyebrows. "I don't believe Megan would ever do anything against Brandon."

"Don't forget she was a woman scorned," Jenny reminded her. "We don't know what happened between them. Maybe they had a really bad breakup."

"You haven't seen Megan mooning around Brandon like I have," Heather argued. "She's had her eye on him for years. It's easier to believe she was working on getting him back."

"So you don't think she was really friendly with Kelly?"

"Would you be?" Heather asked. "Brandon is the love of her life. Why would she want to go shopping with the woman who's taken her place?"

Jenny was quiet while she processed what Heather said.

"Maybe I'm looking at it all wrong," she said. "What if Megan was hounding Kelly? Forcing her to do something for her?"

"We'll never know that now," Heather pointed out.

"The whole idea is farfetched anyway," Jenny sighed. "We need to talk to Brandon."

"Let's go see him now," Heather said. "Star can take care of the café."

"She's been helping me a lot lately," Jenny said. "She barely has time to paint. I feel bad, imposing on her so much."

"She's doing it because she loves you," Heather said.

Jenny reflected over her good fortune. When her husband left her for another woman, she had been alone and forlorn. Coming to Pelican Cove had been the best decision of her life. She had reconnected with her aunt and met the Magnolias. The group of women provided a strong support system for Jenny and she felt touched by their unconditional love.

Jenny called the café on her cell phone and spoke to her aunt. She drove to the Newbury estate, hoping Brandon would be in a better mood.

Both girls heaved a sigh of relief when they learned Ada Newbury was out. The maid led them out to the beach. Brandon was out for a run. They could see him in the distance.

"Looks like he's getting back to normal," Heather said.

Brandon spotted them and waved. They waited until he jogged up to them. Brandon picked up a towel from a chair and wiped the sweat off his face and hands.

"Nice day for a run," he said, picking up a glass of juice and draining it in a gulp.

The maid came back with a tray loaded with refreshments. Brandon played the gracious host and insisted they taste the assortment of cookies before them. Jenny sipped the freshly squeezed lemonade and felt energized.

"What brings you here, ladies?" Brandon asked.

"More questions," Jenny said. "I hope you don't mind."

"You can ask me anything you want." Brandon was solicitous. "I hope you will find out what happened to Kelly. It won't bring her back but at least it will give me some closure."

"It's about Megan and Kelly," Jenny explained. "Did you find it odd that they got along so well together?"

Brandon looked surprised.

"Why would I?" he asked. "Kelly knew Megan before she met me."

"What?" Heather and Jenny cried out together.

"I met Kelly at a party thrown by Megan," Brandon said. "We hit it off right away. Megan had already dumped me at that time, so I was free to see whoever I wanted. We went on our first date the next day, Kelly and I."

"Did you ever ask Megan how she knew Kelly?"

Brandon shook his head.

"Never thought about it."

Heather chatted with Brandon for a while and the girls took their leave.

"Back to Megan's?" Heather asked as Jenny started the car.

Jenny nodded grimly. She tried to remember all the questions she had asked Megan. Had she ever asked Megan when she first met Kelly?

Megan didn't hide her displeasure when she opened the door and saw them standing outside.

"What now?"

"We just have some follow-up questions," Jenny said, refusing to back down. "You can talk to us or talk to the police."

"You can't threaten me like that," Megan said angrily. "And I don't mind talking to the police. I have nothing to hide."

"Let us come in, then," Heather soothed.

Jenny didn't waste any time.

"When did you first meet Kelly?"

"Didn't we already talk about that?" Megan asked with a frown.

"Tell me again."

"Brandon introduced us. I don't remember the exact date. It was a Sunday and we met for brunch."

"You are sure you didn't know her before that?" Jenny pressed.

"That's not what Brandon says," Heather burst out. "He says you introduced them."

"Impossible," Megan exclaimed. She stared back at Jenny. "Did Brandon really say that?"

Jenny thought back to their conversation with

Brandon, trying to remember his exact words.

"He said he met her at a party you threw."

Megan sighed with relief and laughed nervously.

"Oh! That doesn't mean I knew her."

"Can you explain what you mean by that?" Jenny asked.

"I'm a publicist," Megan began. "I host a lot of parties for my clients. Most of them are high profile people from different walks of life. My job is to invite a selected group of people who can be seen and photographed with my clients. I need to create the right vibe and sometimes I need a crowd of people. I hire people who produce this crowd, youngsters working in the city who like to party. They just come for the free booze. I rarely get to talk to these people."

"You are saying Kelly was one of these freeloaders?"

"She might have been," Megan said emphatically. "My point is, I don't know all the people who come to my parties. Not unless I have invited them myself."

Jenny marveled over how ironic the situation was. Megan had unwittingly played a part in bringing Brandon and Kelly together.

# Chapter 12

Jenny scooped some mashed avocado on slices of smoked turkey and squirted her special chipotle mayo on top. She folded the wrap and set it on a platter.

Star tossed pasta and diced vegetables in fresh basil pesto.

"Did you post the turkey wraps on Instagram?" she asked Jenny. "The tourists are going to love them."

"You think so?" Jenny asked, furrowing her brow.

Jenny's creative recipes had made the Boardwalk Café a roaring success. But she was still hesitant before introducing any new items on the menu.

"Didn't you want to talk to Adam?" Star asked. "Why don't you go now?"

Jenny made a few dozen wraps and put them in the refrigerator. She grabbed two wraps and a small container of salad for Adam and walked to the police station.

Pelican Cove was enjoying another warm, spring day. Jenny gazed up at the sky and closed her eyes, breathing in the salty air.

A big pile of files littered Adam's desk. He didn't look too happy to see Jenny.

"Isn't it early for lunch?" he asked, spying the basket Jenny carried on her arm.

"You can eat it later," Jenny told him. "I'm going to put this in the refrigerator out in the galley."

"Thanks, Jenny," Adam smiled. "That's kind of you."

Jenny stood her ground.

"Is there anything else?" Adam sighed.

"Do you have Kelly's phone records?" Jenny asked. "We never talked about them."

"And we are not going to," Adam snorted. "I have a busy day ahead, Jenny."

Jenny took the hint and walked out of Adam's office. The phone records would have to wait.

The Magnolias had arrived for their mid-morning break by the time Jenny got back to the Boardwalk Café.

Betty Sue stared at something while her hands moved in a rhythm, knitting something green. Molly barely paid attention to the book in her hand. Heather was busy snapping pictures on her phone. Jenny wondered what the women were so engrossed in.

Then she noticed her aunt. Star held a bundle wrapped in pink in her arms.

"Is that Emily?" Jenny squealed as she ran up the café steps.

She looked down at the baby her aunt held and made kissing noises. The cherub gurgled and looked back at her with large brown eyes.

"Emily's spending some time with us," Star said. "Jason is running some errands."

The baby let out a cry, signaling she needed to be changed. Jenny took her inside and clumsily changed her diaper. She hadn't done that since her son grew up.

Emily sat in her stroller, chewing her fists, drooling and smiling at the Magnolias.

Jenny poured coffee for everyone and brought out a plate of muffins.

"Is Ada treating you well?" Betty Sue asked Jenny. "You let me know if she gets too hoity toity. You are doing her a favor. Don't you let her forget it."

"Don't worry about me, Betty Sue," Jenny assured her. "I'm not bothered about Ada."

"Found anything new?" Molly asked.

Jenny shook her head.

"I don't seem to have any clear leads."

"That pool boy is highly suspicious," Heather said, setting her phone aside.

She had clicked a few dozen pictures of the baby.

"Who, Enrique?" Jenny asked. "Why do you suspect him, Heather?"

"Have you looked at him?" Heather asked, fanning herself. "He's so hot it's got to be a crime."

Betty Sue cleared her throat and looked flushed.

"Didn't he say he was sleeping the night of the party?" Molly asked.

"That's what he says," Heather nodded. "But do we really believe him? He's the only person who could have let Kelly into the pool house."

"So you think he's been lying to us all this time?" Jenny asked.

"Why not?" Heather asked. "You have no reason to trust him, Jenny."

"Say he let Kelly in that night," Jenny said. "What do

you think happened?"

"They fought over something?" Heather said. "This Kelly seems like a loose character. Maybe she came on to Enrique and he snubbed her. Or it could have been the other way around. What if Enrique got fresh with Kelly?"

Jenny continued Heather's line of thought.

"They had a tussle. Enrique pushed Kelly into the pool. Or she could have slipped and fallen in herself."

"Why didn't he pull her out?" Molly asked.

"He didn't realize she was drowning?" Jenny spoke out loud. "He might have walked away and never realized what was happening behind his back."

Heather's face darkened as she thought of the alternative.

"Or he stood there and let Kelly die."

"That would make him a cold blooded murderer," Jenny said with a shudder. "Why would Enrique do that?"

"Revenge?" Star offered. "Didn't you say Kelly rejected his advances?"

"That's just one of my theories," Jenny sighed.

"Enrique insists it was the other way round."

"He could have been working for someone else," Heather offered.

"You mean like a hired killer?" Jenny asked. "This is beginning to sound fantastic."

The baby had fallen asleep while the women talked. Star covered her with an extra blanket, making sure she was warm enough.

"What if Ada Newbury hired the pool boy to kill that poor girl?" Star asked.

Jenny's mouth dropped open.

"She wouldn't go that far," she said hoarsely.

Betty Sue was shaking her head from side to side, too shocked at Star's suggestion to say anything.

"She does have a motive," Molly offered. "We know Mrs. Newbury wasn't happy with the wedding. Clearly, she didn't want her grandson marrying Kelly."

"We know she tried to bribe Kelly," Heather mused. "Maybe she didn't stop there."

"I am sure Ada was fast asleep in her bed at midnight," Betty Sue insisted.

She and Ada were staunch rivals and rarely saw eye to eye. So the Magnolias were surprised to see her defend Ada.

"You have given me an idea," Jenny told Betty Sue. "I never asked Ada about her alibi."

"Let's go talk to her now," Heather said eagerly.

"Hello ladies!" a cheerful voice hailed them from the boardwalk.

Jason Stone walked up, holding a few grocery bags in his hands. He came up the café steps and rushed to the baby's stroller.

"Shhh …" Star said, placing a finger on her lips.

"Isn't she an angel?" Jason gushed.

He set his bags down and collapsed into a chair. Jenny offered him a muffin.

"I'm too tired to eat," Jason groaned. "In fact, I'm exhausted."

He tipped his head at the baby in the stroller.

"This little lady's been keeping me up at night."

"Have you thought of getting a nanny?" Betty Sue asked.

"I'm not too keen on that," Jason said. "I want to take care of her myself."

"We are here to help," Star said, patting him on the arm.

Jason let out a big yawn. He told them how he had driven around Pelican Cove for hours the previous night with Emily in her car seat.

"She would nod off while the car was moving, and start crying as soon as the car stopped."

"Nick was like that," Jenny said, remembering. "I used to wear a hole in the carpet, walking him around the house. He would start wailing the moment I set him down."

They talked about Emily for a few minutes. Jason finally stood up and headed home with his baby.

"Shall we go now?" Heather reminded Jenny.

"Let's make sure Ada's home," Jenny said.

Ada was expected back home in an hour. Star forced them to stay back and have lunch before they went out.

"Ada won't like being questioned," Heather said as they drove into the hills where the Newbury estate was situated.

"When does she like anything I say?" Jenny shrugged. "I need to ask the tough questions."

Ada Newbury was entertaining her golf coach in the parlor.

"We just got back from a lesson," she enthused. "Coach says I am improving a lot."

She looked admiringly at the tall man who sat sprawled in a delicate chair.

"She's really been working on her swing," the man spoke. "I wish all my students were that dedicated."

"Zac, right?" Jenny greeted the man. She turned to look at Ada. "Can I have a word with you, Mrs. Newbury?"

Ada looked longingly at the golf pro.

"Zac has to leave for another lesson."

Zac Gordon stood up and stretched himself. He patted Ada on the shoulder and took his leave.

"What brings you here today?" Ada asked tersely.

Jenny was direct.

"We never talked about your alibi. What were you doing around midnight the night of the party?"

"What do you think I was doing?" Ada shot back. "I must have been in bed."

"Were you?" Jenny asked.

"Of course I was," Ada said.

"Can someone vouch for it?"

"Julius is out of town," Ada said, referring to her husband. "I was alone."

"Are you ready to swear you never left your room that night?" Jenny asked.

"You're out of line," Ada scowled. "Are you actually suspecting me?"

"You did have a motive," Jenny pointed out. "And you argued with Kelly that night."

"That doesn't mean I'm guilty," Ada said.

Jenny didn't back down.

"I'm not saying you are. I just want to know where you were that night, and what you were doing."

"I don't want to talk about it," Ada said.

"As you wish," Jenny said with a shrug. "But you're holding me back."

She walked out of the house with Heather close behind. One of the maids came hurrying out while they were getting into the car. Jenny didn't recognize her.

"Are you the one who's asking questions about the party?" the girl asked.

"What's up?" Jenny asked, nodding affirmatively.

"You know Enrique, the pool boy?" the girl asked. "I saw him on the beach just when the party was winding down."

"But …" Heather butted in.

Jenny held up her hand, warning Heather to stay quiet.

"What was he doing there?"

"He was drinking," the girl said. "Must have filched a bottle from the bar."

"Was he alone?" Jenny asked.

"He was, at first. Then Mr. Brandon's girl walked up to him."

"You mean Kelly?" Jenny asked. "The girl who died?"

"That's right," the maid nodded. "Enrique was shaking his head while he talked to her. Then he laughed at her. She stomped off."

"What time was this?" Heather asked.

"Some time after 11," the girl said. "At least that's what I think. But I'm not sure."

"Thanks for letting us know," Jenny told the girl.

The girl smiled shyly and hurried back inside.

Jenny and Heather stared at each other, speechless.

"I told you not to trust that stud muffin," Heather burst out. "So he's been lying to us all this time."

"I don't know, Heather." Jenny was skeptical. "How do we know it's not the maid who lied to us? I mean, where was she all this time? Why did she come forward now?"

"You have a soft spot for that pool boy," Heather said, rolling her eyes. "He's worked his magic on you, hasn't he?"

"Don't be ridiculous," Jenny snapped. "I'm just trying to be objective."

"Doesn't look like that to me."

The girls bickered over whether the pool boy was guilty or not on the way back to town.

"One thing's odd," Jenny said, trying to calm down.

"Kelly seems to have had an argument with multiple people. She fought with Ada. Now we learn she fought with the pool boy. She was sending all those messages to Paula. What in the world was this girl up to?"

"Don't forget she was probably having an affair too," Heather said vehemently. "I'm starting to believe Ada. Kelly wasn't kosher. She was bad for Brandon."

"It's beginning to look that way," Jenny agreed. "But did Brandon know the truth about Kelly?"

# Chapter 13

The Boardwalk Café was packed. Tourists and locals sat elbow to elbow, enjoying Jenny's lunch special.

"I'm not a curry fan," Barb Norton, a short, stout woman said. "But I could eat this shrimp curry every day."

Jenny hurried from table to table, making sure everyone was well looked after.

"Allow yourself a pat on the back," Star beamed. "This shrimp curry is going to make you famous."

"More famous than she already is, you mean," Heather said.

She had posted pictures of Jenny's special shrimp curry on social media. Fans of the Boardwalk Café had called for reservations, not wanting to miss the limited time item on the menu.

"You might have to make this curry a regular feature," Betty Sue said. "And why not? We have access to the freshest shrimp."

Jenny drank in all the praise with a smile on her face. Her mind was whirling with other thoughts. Ada Newbury was still under suspicion. The police hadn't made much progress, and neither had she. Jenny wondered what the missing link was.

She hadn't had much help from Adam. She had tried to make him talk when they went out for dinner the previous night. But Adam didn't have much to say. He had admitted he was stumped. They needed a break and soon.

Jenny thought about what to do next and remembered Kelly's phone. Were the police still waiting on her phone records? She would have to talk to Adam again.

Adam Hopkins himself walked into the café a few minutes later.

"What are you doing here?" Jenny asked in surprise.

"This is your moment of triumph," he said, planting a kiss on her forehead. "I wasn't going to miss it."

Jenny's eyes widened in surprise. Adam wasn't fond of showing affection in public. A stranger looking at them wouldn't know they were an engaged couple.

"You've already tasted the curry!" Jenny exclaimed.

She had cooked at least a dozen test batches until she perfected her recipe.

"Who says I can't enjoy it again?" Adam asked with a smile.

Jenny led him out to the deck. It was a beautiful spring day in Pelican Cove. Warm afternoon sunshine bathed the tables. The air smelt salty and the breeze blowing over the ocean was cool and pleasant.

"One shrimp curry coming up," Jenny said cheerfully.

"Why don't you join me?" Adam asked, when Jenny brought out his order herself.

"Why don't you get started?" Jenny asked apologetically. "I need to be out front for a little while more."

"I'll be waiting," Adam said, picking up his fork with gusto.

Jenny accepted many compliments from her customers and promised them she would make the shrimp curry a weekly feature.

Star and Heather pushed her out on the deck after the crowd thinned.

"Go sit with that young man of yours," Star said. "And grab a bite to eat."

Adam's face lit up when Jenny sat down before him.

"I have some news," Adam said, scraping the last bit of rice and curry from his plate.

Jenny waited while he savored his mouthful. She crossed her fingers and waited for him to speak.

"Kelly's phone records came back," Adam said, dabbing his mouth with a tissue. "We already know who she was calling or talking to. I was more interested in finding out where she has been."

"What did you find?" Jenny asked, holding her breath.

"Her phone was in the same location as Paula's several times."

"We need to find out who Kelly was with both before and during the party," Jenny said. "Who did she spend a lot of time with apart from Brandon?"

Neither of them had an answer for that.

"We have hit a wall again," Adam said, getting up.

Jenny saw Adam off and started helping her aunt clear up.

"What's that frown for?" Heather asked, drying dishes with a towel. "Did you and Adam have a fight again?"

"I'm thinking of Kelly," Jenny admitted. "We need to find out more about her life in the city."

"Only one way to do that," Heather said with a grin. "Go to the source."

"Are you angling for a road trip, Heather?" Jenny asked, rolling her eyes.

"Think about it. It's been ages since we had some fun. We can do some sleuthing and hit that Mexican restaurant you like so much."

"What about Molly?"

"She's getting off early today," Heather informed Jenny. "It's the perfect day for a trip to the city."

Heather called Brandon and asked him for Kelly's address in the city. Kelly had shared an apartment with two other girls. Jenny knew the area well.

Molly was excited when they picked her up.

"This trip is long overdue," she said as she climbed into Jenny's car.

The girls cranked up the radio and sang at the top of their voices as the car sped across the miles. The sun was just setting as they entered the city. The roads were clogged with commuters heading home. A pink haze shrouded the city and restaurants filled with people meeting for drinks or dinner.

"I'm starving," Heather complained.

"Didn't you have two helpings of the curry?" Jenny teased. "Let's get to work first, ladies. You gotta sing for your supper, you know."

Getting to Kelly's apartment took them longer than expected. Jenny drove through a pair of imposing gates and parked before the leasing office. A young man was busy mowing the lawn. He pointed out Kelly's apartment building. It was a two storied structure with eight units. Kelly's turned out to be the one at the back on the second floor. Jenny pressed the doorbell and hoped someone was home.

"Who are you?" a heavily made up girl asked as she opened the door a crack.

Jenny eyed the tiny gold dress she wore, too low at the top and too high at the bottom. She was very obviously dressed to go out and party.

"Is this Kelly's apartment?" Jenny asked.

The girl nodded and narrowed her eyes suspiciously.

"We are Kelly's friends," Jenny explained. "We wanted to grab something from her closet."

The girl's eyes widened as she connected the dots. She finally opened the door and invited them in.

The apartment was clean and well furnished. The girl pointed to a closed door situated to the right of the living room.

"That's Kelly's room. She shared it with another girl."

"How many girls live here?" Heather asked.

"It's a two bedroom apartment," the girl bragged. "There's four of us on the lease. We rent out our couch sometimes."

Jenny, Heather and Molly stared at the girl.

"This place is expensive!" the girl said defensively. "Everyone knows that."

Jenny agreed with the girl and talked passionately about rising apartment rents. Heather and Molly went into Kelly's room and started rooting around in her closet. Heather took her time, giving Jenny a chance to talk with the girl.

"How long did you know Kelly?"

"We've been roomies for a couple of years," the girl replied. "But we hardly saw each other."

"Oh?"

"I work the night shift," the girl explained. "So does another girl who lives here. That's why we didn't step on each other's toes. We were hardly here at the same time."

"So you never met Brandon?" Jenny asked innocently.

"Who's Brandon?" the girl asked.

"Her fiancé."

"Kelly was a sly one, wasn't she? She ditched the tall hunk."

"Was Kelly dating someone?" Jenny asked.

The girl assumed a knowing look.

"Tall, dark haired hunk with a six pack. You could bounce a ball off those abs."

Jenny tried to visualize Brandon Newbury. The kindest person wouldn't call him tall. He certainly didn't have a flat stomach.

"Did she introduce this tall guy as her boyfriend?"

"He spent a lot of time here," the girl said suggestively. "Behind that door, if you know what I mean."

"Did Kelly break up with this guy?" Jenny asked curiously.

"I couldn't say either way," the girl said with a shrug. "Look, we weren't that close. Kelly kept to herself."

"Do you know this guy's name?" Jenny asked.

"His name was Paul, although Kelly called him something else. It was a silly nickname. I don't remember."

Heather and Molly came out of the room, holding a couple of dresses.

"Thanks for letting us in," she told the girl.

"Where is Kelly's funeral?" the girl asked. "Me and the other girls might try to make it."

Jenny noted the girl's phone number and promised to send her the details.

Heather and Molly declared they were dying of thirst.

"I want a tall frozen margarita," Molly sighed. "With plenty of salt on the rim."

"I thought you were driving," Jenny groaned.

"No way," Heather and Molly both cried out.

Jenny agreed to be the designated driver under protest.

"You can still have something frozen," Molly consoled and yowled when Jenny punched her in the shoulder.

The girls had started on their second basket of chips and salsa when Heather finally mentioned Kelly.

"Did you learn anything new?"

"I'm not sure what I learnt," Jenny said, scooping up

some guacamole with a warm tortilla chip.

She told the girls about the tall, handsome guy who Kelly had been going around with.

"Brandon's good looking but even I wouldn't call him tall," Heather declared. "Does this confirm Kelly was two timing Brandon?"

"Looks that way," Jenny nodded. "But who is this mysterious tall guy?"

"Did you get his name?" Molly asked.

"The girl said he was called Paul," Jenny said.

Then she clamped a hand on her mouth and stared at the girls.

"Paul, Paul-a. It's like Betty Sue said. Paula is actually a man."

"It can't be that obvious," Heather said, shaking her head.

The waitress brought over their order. The girls had opted for different types of enchiladas. Heather cut into the melted cheese and argued with Jenny.

"So Kelly was calling and messaging this guy in front of Brandon? And he never caught on?"

"We know this Paula person was in Pelican Cove," Jenny said, her food forgotten. "Who could it be?"

"Didn't you mention Kelly was hanging around with some guy on the night of the party?" Molly asked, swallowing a big bite.

She had never met Kelly since she hadn't been invited to the party. But she had a strong memory and she remembered the girls talking about how Brandon and Kelly had both spent the evening with other people instead of each other.

"That was her cousin," Jenny dismissed.

Then she thought again. Could it be?

"Is it possible?" she asked out loud.

"You don't think Binkie was her boyfriend?" Heather asked, alarmed.

"Think of how she was clinging to him that night."

"Surely she wasn't that shameless?" Heather cried. "You're saying she paraded her boyfriend around at her own wedding party? Right in front of the man she was supposedly going to marry?"

"He was supposed to be her cousin," Jenny said slowly. "Why would anyone suspect them?"

Heather ate a big bite and put down her fork.

"He was quite handsome," she said. "And tall. Much taller than Brandon. And Binkie can't be his real name."

"So Binkie and Paul are the same," Jenny summed up. "And he was either Kelly's ex or she was still seeing him on the side."

"Do you think Brandon knew about him?" Heather asked, feeling sorry for her cousin.

"I hope not," Jenny sighed. "It gives him a very strong motive."

# Chapter 14

Jenny primped before the mirror, excited about her dinner date with Adam. He was taking her to a new restaurant in a nearby town.

Star sat in a chair in Jenny's room, looking at her indulgently.

"Are you going to talk about setting a date?"

"I told you, we are not in a hurry," Jenny said, fastening a diamond stud.

"That boy needs a nudge," Star said. "He won't make a move on his own."

Star ignored her niece's protests and decided to drop a few hints when she saw Adam again.

"Whatever you do, don't talk about the murder," Star advised. "Don't spoil the mood."

"What mood is that?" Jenny asked with a laugh.

"Try to be more romantic, Jenny," Star clucked. "Stay away from hot button issues."

"There is no such thing," Jenny said patiently.

"Of course there is," Star protested. "Don't talk about

Jason, for instance."

"Why not?" Jenny asked, surprised.

"The whole town knows Jason is in love with you," Star sighed. "Adam knows it too, Jenny. And he's jealous."

"That's silly," Jenny said. "I chose him, didn't I?"

"I still think Jason is the better man for you," Star said hopefully.

Star was very fond of Jason Stone. She had tried to push her niece toward the jovial, kind hearted lawyer but Jenny's heart had chosen Adam, the cranky, brooding sheriff.

"No more of that, Auntie," Jenny warned.

"You're spending too much time with Jason," Star continued. "People are beginning to talk. Adam's noticed it too."

"I'm spending time with Emily," Jenny said. Her face lit up as she thought of Jason's baby girl. "Adam knows I am in love with that sweet baby."

"What about her father?" Star asked, quirking an eyebrow.

Jenny ignored her aunt and ran a brush through her

hair. The doorbell chimed below and she skipped down the steps, looking forward to her date.

Adam stood outside the door, carrying an armful of red roses. Jenny put them in a vase and took Adam's arm. The moon was rising over the ocean, lighting up the sky as they drove out of town.

"How was your day?" Jenny asked Adam. "Anything interesting happen?"

"Let's not talk about work," Adam said.

Jenny agreed readily. The next three hours passed pleasantly. Jenny enjoyed a chardonnay from a local winery and dug into her lobster ravioli with gusto. Adam declared the spaghetti and meatballs he had ordered were the best he had ever eaten. They had passion fruit gelato for dessert. Jenny sighed happily as she sipped her coffee. Adam had a rare smile on his face.

Jenny was drowsy on the drive back home. She barely paid attention when Adam started talking about Kelly.

"I think this clears Ada Newbury."

"What? What was that?" Jenny asked, snapping awake.

"Paul Briggs is a more likely suspect."

"Who's Paul Briggs?" Jenny asked, stifling a yawn.

"Haven't you heard anything I just said?" Adam asked.

Jenny admitted she might have dozed off. She blamed it on the excellent meal they had just indulged in.

"We brought Paul Briggs in for questioning today," Adam began again. "He says he is Kelly's ex-boyfriend but I believe they were still seeing each other."

"That's Binkie, right? The guy who was parading as Kelly's cousin?"

"You knew about that?" Adam asked.

"I wasn't sure until now. Why didn't Kelly break it off with Brandon if she was still involved with this guy?"

"It was all part of their plan," Adam explained. "They were going to dupe Brandon."

"How?"

"He was sketchy about the details. But they were playing a long game. I think Kelly was going to marry Brandon and then divorce him a few days later, getting a big settlement or alimony."

"Not very original," Jenny offered.

"No," Adam agreed. "Briggs readily admits he was planning to con Brandon. But he is emphatic about being innocent of Kelly's murder. First of all, he loved

Kelly and he wouldn't dream of harming her. More importantly though, she was his meal ticket. Their big pay day depended on the success of this plan."

"Exactly!" Jenny said eagerly. "But what if Kelly changed her mind?"

"She got greedy?"

"Think about it. She came here and saw the Newbury estate. She realized how rich Brandon really was. Why wouldn't she want it all for herself?"

"That would leave this Briggs guy in the lurch."

"So you can't rule him out completely."

Adam banged his hand on the steering wheel and exclaimed in frustration.

Jenny patted his arm.

"Ada's motive looks really weak now, doesn't it? Can I tell her she's in the clear?"

"Go ahead," Adam said grudgingly. "I'm going to focus on these three men now. Brandon, Paul and that pool guy."

Jenny told Adam about Enrique's fake alibi.

"I'm not surprised he lied," Adam said. "I believe he is

capable of doing anything for money."

Jenny wasn't ready for the evening to end. She suggested a walk on the beach and Adam readily agreed. They strolled hand in hand, enjoying the fair weather. Jenny told Adam she was watching Emily the next morning.

"You don't mind, do you?" she asked Adam, watching his face for any sign of aggravation.

"You're spending a lot of time with Jason," Adam said woodenly.

"Jason and I will always be friends," Jenny said. There was a note of censure in her voice. "Emily's just a baby, Adam."

"Better than traipsing around, getting into trouble," Adam muttered. He cleared his throat and said meekly, "I didn't know you liked babies."

"Of course I love babies. Who doesn't? And Emily is such a dear. She hardly ever cries."

Adam deftly changed the topic. They had reached an unspoken truce by the time they got back to the house. Jenny spotted Jason's car in the driveway and rushed in.

Star was pacing the living room, carrying Emily in her arms. Jason sat in an armchair, looking frazzled. Jenny noticed he was dressed in pajamas.

"What's wrong?" she burst out. "Is Emily sick?"

Star widened her eyes and shook her head, warning Jenny to be quiet.

Adam had come in after Jenny. He took in the whole scene at a glance. He tipped his head when he caught Jenny's eye and walked out. Jenny deduced he would catch up with her later.

Jenny sat down next to Jason, her eyes following her aunt across the room.

"I'm sorry," Jason whispered. "She started crying hours ago and just wouldn't stop. I didn't know what to do."

"I'm glad you came here," Jenny whispered back. "She'll be fine. Don't worry."

The baby finally fell asleep half an hour later.

"What if she starts crying again?" Star asked. "Spend the night here. We'll take good care of this little missy."

Jason stayed over at Seaview, too tired to argue with Jenny and Star.

Next morning, Jenny yawned all the way to the Boardwalk Café. She had woken up thrice to change the baby and feed her. A bank of heavy, storm filled clouds hovered over the shore, blotting out any light from the rising sun.

Jenny baked a few batches of muffins and diced vegetables and ham for western omelets. Two hours later, she finally pulled her apron off and sat down in the kitchen to take a break. Star had arrived an hour earlier.

Heather Morse walked in, looking for Jenny.

"Did you know they arrested Binkie?" she asked in a rush.

"I think they just questioned him." Jenny told her everything she had learned from Adam.

"This gets more confusing every day," Heather groaned. "Are we ever going to find out what happened to Kelly?"

Jenny didn't have an answer for that.

"At least Ada Newbury is not a suspect anymore," she said. "I want to go and give her the good news."

"Lead me on," Heather said cheerfully. "I've finished all my chores for the day."

Jenny neglected calling for an appointment. She assembled a big platter of chicken salad sandwiches for lunch and promised her aunt she would be back at the earliest.

"How can I ever thank you enough?" she asked Star.

"Stop worrying about me and get out of here," Star said.

The two girls set off in Jenny's car under an overcast sky. Heather regaled Jenny with an account of the tremendous response her shrimp curry was getting on Instagram.

"People who tried it can't stop talking about it," Heather said, smiling broadly. "They want to come back and bring their friends."

"It's a simple recipe, really," Jenny said modestly.

"I know what you should do," Heather said eagerly. "Have cooking sessions. Like those master classes they show on TV. You'll be sold out."

"I suppose it will be good advertising for the café," Jenny mused. "It's a great idea, Heather. I'm going to think about it."

They stopped at the gates when they reached the Newbury estate. The guards did their thing. Jenny handed over a bag of muffins, raising a smile out of a big, sullen guard.

Ada Newbury wasn't too pleased to see them.

"I have a golf lesson in half an hour," she said, frowning at her wrist watch. "You should really call before you come."

"This won't take long," Jenny said, refusing to be affected by Ada's grumpiness.

Ada led them into the parlor. Jenny and Heather sat down without an invitation, forcing Ada to take a seat.

"You're in the clear, Mrs. Newbury," Jenny informed Ada. "The police don't think you had anything to do with Kelly's death."

"I could have told them that," Ada quipped.

Jenny hadn't expected any compliments from Ada. But she couldn't help being a bit disappointed.

"So my work here is done?"

"Do you know who killed that girl?" Ada asked.

"That hasn't been determined yet," Jenny said.

"I want you to keep looking," Ada said. "I can pay you anything you want."

Jenny herself was curious to find out what had happened to Kelly. She had been thinking of continuing her search anyway.

"I thought you didn't like Kelly," she said. "Why do you care what happened to her?"

"I didn't like the girl for a reason," she said. "She was wrong for my Brandon. I'm sure she was just taking advantage of him."

Jenny knew that was true. She told Ada what they had found out about Kelly.

"So I'm not senile yet," Ada said triumphantly. "My instincts do mean something. My poor boy! He's well rid of this nuisance."

Although Jenny thought Ada was being harsh, she couldn't help but agree with her.

"How is Brandon doing?" Heather asked.

"Don't tell him about this other guy," Ada warned. "Who knows how he will react."

"I think Brandon knew Kelly was involved with someone," Jenny said.

"Then why didn't he boot the girl out of here?" Ada asked, shocked.

"I guess he loved her too much," Heather said.

"Love!" Ada spat. "Love means nothing without honor. Honor and respect. And whatever happened to trust? I couldn't love a person I don't trust."

Heather and Jenny listened to Ada's tirade with their heads down. They knew she was right this time. Neither of them could say anything to console her.

Zac Gordon walked into the parlor. Jenny hadn't known he was around.

"Zac's giving me a ride to the club," Ada said curtly.

Jenny and Heather thought about the fleet of luxury cars housed in the big garage outside. They couldn't help but exchange a look.

What was Zac doing there?

Zac's hair was wet and looked like it had been finger combed. He greeted the girls cheerfully.

"Nothing like a swim to recharge you," he said. "When are you coming to the club?" he asked Jenny. "I have a long waitlist but I can make an exception for you."

"Jenny doesn't belong to the country club," Ada said haughtily. "She will need someone to sign her in as a guest."

"I told you I can sneak you in," Zac told Jenny with a wink. "Just say when."

Ada was getting impatient.

"Is it too late for our lesson?" Ada asked Zac apologetically. "These girls turned up without an appointment."

"The lesson begins whenever you are ready," Zac said smoothly, taking Ada's hand.

They walked out together, hand in hand. Zac bent down to whisper something in Ada's ear, making her giggle.

Jenny and Heather watched them go, feeling bewildered. Ada Newbury never giggled.

# Chapter 15

The Magnolias sat on the windswept deck of the Boardwalk Café and exclaimed over Jenny's latest parfait. It was made with strawberry yogurt, macadamia nuts and toasted coconut flakes. There were generous layers of plump, juicy strawberries in between.

"I'm beginning to take a shine to these," Betty Sue said, licking her spoon.

A small storm was brewing and the waves lashed against the shore with more than usual force.

"We are getting a lot of rain this year," Star grumbled. "I have hardly ever been out painting."

"That's my fault," Jenny owned up. "You have been stuck here, helping me out."

"Tell us about your trip to Ada's," Molly said. "Did she at least thank you for your efforts?"

"She wants me to keep looking," Jenny sighed. "I'm not sure if I can help. Every time I think I'm on to something, it turns out to be a dead end."

Heather looked up from her phone.

"Remember what that maid told us about Enrique?"

"The pool boy?" Molly asked with a hint of mischief. "Are you looking for a chance to meet him again?"

"He's barely legal," Heather sighed. "Just a boy, really."

"What about Enrique?" Jenny asked, ignoring their banter.

"He lied to us about being asleep. The maid saw him walking around."

"She might have been mistaken," Jenny reasoned.

"Why don't we ask him outright?"

Jenny's face set in a frown.

"If he lied to us the first time, what makes you think he won't lie to us again?"

"Second time's the charm?" Heather asked hopefully. "Anyway, I fancy a swim. Are you coming?"

"Isn't it too cold?" Molly asked.

"Doesn't matter," Heather supplied. "It's a heated pool."

Jenny stole a glance at her aunt. She didn't want to lean on her aunt and take off again.

"A swim sounds perfect," Star said, reading Jenny's mind. "It will perk you up."

"But ..." Jenny began.

"Go! Don't worry about me."

Jenny insisted on helping her aunt get ready for lunch. She stirred a big pot of vegetable barley soup as she made her mint and parsley pesto. She made pesto chicken and sweet pepper sandwiches for the lunch special. An hour later, Star literally pushed her out of the kitchen.

Heather had gone home to get her swimming things. She stood out on deck, waiting impatiently for Jenny to get going.

Jenny drove into the hills toward the Newbury estate. The girls took the path that skirted the main house and walked directly to the pool house.

"How do we get in?" Jenny asked as they stood before the access panel.

"Enrique will let us in," Heather shrugged, pushing the button that acted as a doorbell. "Or I will call Brandon and ask for the code."

"Maybe we should just go back if Enrique is not here," Jenny said uncertainly.

She wasn't keen on getting an earful from Ada Newbury.

"We are here for a swim," Heather said stoutly. "Just relax, Jenny. Don't worry about that old trout."

"Hush Heather," Jenny warned, looking over her shoulder.

She admitted to herself that she was jittery. She didn't know why.

Enrique ambled out of the pool house and grinned when he saw them. He punched in the code to unlock the gate. Heather rushed in, waving cheerfully at Enrique.

"Great day for a swim, huh?"

Five minutes later, Heather and Jenny were swimming laps in the pool. Enrique sat in a chair on the patio, looking bored.

"What's he doing, watching us like a creep?" Heather wondered.

"He doubles as a lifeguard," Jenny reminded her. "He's just doing his job."

She swam a few laps and decided she was sadly out of shape. The girls floated on a couple of rafts for some time and finally climbed out of the pool.

"We should do that more often," Heather said eagerly. "I feel so energized."

Enrique got to his feet and beckoned them inside. He pointed to an array of soda cans in the refrigerator. Jenny and Heather both chose one.

"Are you a habitual liar?" Jenny asked casually. "Or do you just have a bad memory?"

"What?" Enrique asked, looking cool as a cucumber.

Heather joined in.

"You told us you were drunk and asleep the night Kelly died. But you were seen walking on the beach that night."

"That's not all," Jenny added. "You talked to Kelly. I think you had a fight with her."

"I never met Kelly that night," Enrique stressed. "I don't know where you are getting your information. But someone's obviously leading you on."

"How do we know you are not the one doing that?"

Enrique shrugged.

"What can you do? You just have to trust me."

"We don't really know you," Heather said, crushing

her soda can. "Why should we believe you?"

Enrique muttered an oath.

"Believe me or don't believe me. I don't care. I have to go now."

He buttoned his shirt and strode out of the pool complex, acting as if he didn't have a care in the world.

"He's just putting on an act," Jenny said, her hands on her hips. "I'm sure he's lying to us."

"Have the police talked to him yet?" Heather asked. "What do they say?"

"I don't know," Jenny replied. "I can ask Adam."

Jenny didn't get a chance to talk to Adam until later that evening. She had invited him home for dinner.

"What's on your mind?" Adam asked as she served him a big steak of fish.

"Enrique," Jenny admitted. "What do you think about him?"

"Do we have to talk about this now?" Adam grumbled. "Can't we have a single meal without you trying to pump me for information?"

Jenny apologized. She knew Adam would clam up if he

was angry. She didn't broach the subject again until they were sitting out on the patio. The big stone fountain gurgled merrily and Adam sat with an arm around her shoulder. The storm had moved past Pelican Cove and a bright moon shone in a clear sky.

"We questioned that pool boy," Adam volunteered. "He doesn't have a strong alibi. But he doesn't have a motive either. He has nothing to gain by harming Kelly."

"I think he's hiding something," Jenny insisted.

They talked about their kids after that. Adam wanted to know if the kids were coming to Pelican Cove for the spring festival. Jenny didn't know but hoped the kids would turn up for the special weekend. She was looking forward to spending more time with her son.

Jenny got to work at the café the next morning with a firm resolve to stay put. Heather had offered to come and help. Jenny convinced her aunt to take the day off.

It was a Friday and the weekend tourists were beginning to flock to town. A group of suburban moms about Jenny's age occupied a big table. They gushed over Jenny's parfaits and asked for the recipe. Jenny was making shrimp po' boys for lunch.

Adam Hopkins rushed into the café around noon, looking for Jenny. His face was brimming with impatience as he waited out on the deck.

"What is it?" Jenny asked, hurrying out to talk to him.

"You were right about the boy," Adam gushed. "I don't know how you do it, Jenny."

"Did he confess?" Jenny asked with bated breath.

"No such thing," Adam said, shaking his head. "I couldn't stop thinking about him so I ordered my men to search the pool house."

"I thought you already did that."

"Not very well, apparently," Adam cursed. "My men found a key in a gym bag."

"A key?" Jenny was puzzled.

"Let me finish," Adam said. "Luckily, I was familiar with the key. It opens a locker in the local bank. You will never guess what we found."

Jenny waited for Adam to go on.

"A bunch of jewelry," Adam said. "A really expensive string of pearls, a diamond necklace and some emerald earrings."

"Where did they come from?" Jenny asked.

"That's what I would like to know," Adam spat. "The boy maintains they belong to him."

"Can I see these jewels?" Jenny asked.

Adam pulled out his phone and showed her some pictures. Jenny had a good eye for jewelry.

"If these are real, they cost a pretty bundle."

"We got a jeweler to check them out," Adam told her. "These are the real deal."

"Do you think these jewels belong to Kelly?" Jenny asked Adam.

"We thought of that," Adam said. "It seems Kelly was wearing some fine jewels at the party. And she was still wearing them when she drowned."

"That means she wasn't killed for money," Jenny said.

Adam was looking frustrated. Jenny convinced him to stay back and have lunch.

"Don't go after that boy, Jenny," Adam warned her when he left. "Let the police do their job."

"See you later tonight," Jenny said, heading back to the kitchen.

Heather's mouth dropped open when Jenny told her about the jewels in Enrique's locker.

"Who do you think they belong to?"

"Kelly, Ada and Megan are the only women involved here," Jenny said thoughtfully. "Surely Ada wouldn't give away her jewels to the pool boy?"

"Kelly's our best bet," Heather said. "But how do we find out if these jewels belonged to her?"

"We can ask Brandon," Jenny suggested. "Or what about that roommate of hers? That girl we met in the city?"

"Excellent idea," Heather approved. "Did you get her phone number?"

"I don't think Adam will send me those jewelry photos," Jenny reasoned. "What am I going to say to this girl?"

"Just talk to her," Heather said. "She might recognize the jewels from their description."

As it turned out, the girl was very familiar with Kelly's jewels.

"I borrowed those emeralds once," she told Jenny. "Kelly was pretty cool about letting us girls borrow her stuff. She said it was meant to be shown off."

Jenny asked her about the pearls and the diamonds. The girl had borrowed them too.

"Any idea where Kelly keeps them?"

"She took all her bling with her," the friend confirmed. "Said she couldn't get married without her favorite pieces."

Jenny hung up the phone and looked at Heather.

"How did Enrique get his hands on Kelly's jewels?" she wondered.

"Let's go ask him," Heather said, jumping down from the kitchen table.

"Adam kind of warned me not to go and see Enrique," Jenny said meekly.

"What if Enrique comes to see you?" Heather asked, a broad smile lighting up her face.

"Wishful thinking?" Jenny asked.

Heather turned her around and pointed at a spot in the café's dining room. Enrique sat at a table near the window, wringing his hands.

"Are you here for lunch?" Jenny asked a few moments later.

Enrique looked resigned.

"Yes, please. I'll eat whatever you have on hand."

Jenny brought out a sandwich bursting with plump,

deep fried shrimp. She placed it on the table and sat down before Enrique. She let him eat a few bites.

"Why did Kelly give you her jewelry?"

Enrique's eyes popped open. He swallowed a mouthful in haste and looked about to bolt.

"Don't even think about lying again," Jenny warned. "I know about the stuff they found in your locker. I am sure you got it from Kelly."

"Can you keep this between us?" Enrique urged.

"Depends on what you are going to tell me," Jenny said sternly. "Out with it."

Enrique leaned forward and spoke softly.

"I was blackmailing Kelly. I saw her kissing that cousin of hers, what's his name? Bunky or something like that."

"Binkie," Jenny corrected automatically.

"Yeah, him," Enrique nodded. "I threatened to tell Brandon."

"What else did you do?" Jenny asked. "Did you push her into the pool?"

Enrique looked alarmed.

"I had nothing to do with that. You have to believe me."

"You lied to us before," Jenny pointed out.

"Kelly had agreed to pay me a lot more," Enrique said. "The jewels were just a down payment. Why would I kill my golden goose?"

# Chapter 16

The Magnolias gathered for their mid-morning coffee break. Betty Sue and Heather had called ahead saying they would be late because Betty Sue needed to go to the bank. Jenny was pouring the coffee when they came in, Betty Sue looking flustered and red in the face.

"I know what I saw," Betty Sue Morse said indignantly.

She was so distressed she had set her knitting aside. Betty Sue rarely did that.

"Calm down, Grandma," Heather said, stroking her back. "We need to watch your blood pressure."

"Leave me alone, girl!" Betty Sue cried, flinging off Heather's hand. "How could she!"

"Take a deep breath, Betty Sue," Star said, "and start at the beginning."

"Ada Newbury was kissing a man," Betty Sue said again.

"Go Julius!" Star chortled. "So their romance is still going strong."

Julius Newbury was Ada's husband.

"She wasn't kissing Julius," Betty Sue said, her chest heaving. "I never saw the man before."

Jenny laughed. Molly and Star joined her.

"Did you see her too?" Jenny asked Heather.

"I wasn't paying attention," Heather said.

"You must be mistaken, Betty Sue," Jenny said. "Ada's well into her seventies. I don't see her having an affair at this age."

Star added her opinion.

"Forget her age. I can't imagine Ada Newbury developing an affection for anyone."

"It was Ada alright," Betty Sue persisted. "She was driving that fancy car of hers. The man was sitting next to her. They were parked in that little alley behind the bank."

"Kissing a man in broad daylight, that too in the heart of the town?" Star frowned. "That doesn't sound like Ada."

"Can you describe the man, Grandma?" Heather asked.

Betty Sue thought for a few seconds and shook her head.

"I was too shocked to notice."

"The only strange man I have seen around Ada is that golf coach of hers," Heather said. "You don't think she's carrying on with him?"

"Zac Gordon?" Jenny asked incredulously. "He's half her age."

"It's not impossible," Heather said.

Heather had recently been in love with a much older man. She didn't believe age was a barrier for true love.

"It's her private business, I guess," Jenny said.

"But she's cheating on her husband," Betty Sue protested.

"Let them handle it, Betty Sue," Star said diplomatically. "Why should we interfere?"

None of the women really believed that Ada Newbury could be involved with a mere golf pro.

Jason Stone walked down the boardwalk carrying the baby in a carrier. The ladies hailed him and Jenny invited him for a cup of coffee. Heather, Jenny and Molly took turns holding the baby, smiling and blowing kisses at her as she gurgled and smiled.

"When is Emily spending the day with us?" Jenny

asked Jason.

"You're always busy at the café," Jason pointed out. "When do you have the time to take care of my girl?"

"How about Sunday?" Jenny asked. "Spend the day with us. We can have a barbecue in the evening."

She invited the Magnolias for the barbecue. Jason told them how he had set up a crib in his office for Emily.

"I still need to go to the city sometimes though," he said gloomily. "I hate leaving Emily."

Jenny marveled at how easily Jason had stepped into the role of a father. She couldn't imagine Adam doing that. But she had to concede he had raised two daughters on his own after his wife passed away. Then she chided herself for comparing the two men. It wasn't fair to either of them.

The day passed in a blur. Jenny stayed busy making lunch and preparing for the next day. She walked to the seafood market on her way home.

Chris Williams greeted her with a big smile. He and Molly were seeing each other. Chris moonlighted as a part-time realtor and was a kind hearted young man.

"How are you doing, Jenny?" he asked, wrapping up her usual order of whitefish fillets and shrimp.

Jenny chatted with him for a while before heading back.

Jenny and her aunt had a quiet dinner at home. Jenny had pan grilled the fish and made a salad. She put on her sneakers after some time and went for a walk on the beach. A yellow Labrador ran up to her, his tail wagging and put his paws on her chest.

"Tank!" Jenny exclaimed happily, fondling the dog.

She pulled a ball out of her pocket and threw it in the distance.

Adam walked up to her, leaning on his cane. He didn't look very happy.

"You look tired," Jenny murmured. "Have you had dinner? I saved a plate for you."

"I'm not hungry," Adam snapped.

They walked away from the house, Adam unwilling to say a word. Jenny let him brood for a while.

"Do you ever listen to me?" he burst out suddenly. "What am I going to do with you, Jenny?"

"What have I done now?" Jenny asked, her hands on her hips.

"I told you to stay away from that pool boy."

"He came to the café. I didn't go looking for him."

"What did you talk about?" Adam demanded. "Tell me everything right now."

Jenny told Adam how Enrique had been blackmailing Kelly.

"And I bet he didn't stop there."

"I don't think he is involved in Kelly's murder," Jenny said. "He had a lot to gain by keeping her alive."

Adam held Jenny's arms and shook her.

"You need to be more careful, Jenny," he cried. "There's a killer on the loose."

"Why are you so upset, Adam?" Jenny asked. "Has something else happened?"

Adam looked grim when he gave Jenny the news.

"Paul Briggs is dead."

"Binkie's dead?" Jenny echoed.

"They found him in his room at the country club," Adam reported. "Don't know why he was still hanging around town."

"What happened to him?" Jenny asked.

"Don't know for sure. My guess is he was poisoned."

"Who would do that?"

"Isn't that the big question?" Adam growled. "Until we catch the culprit, everyone is under suspicion."

"What does anyone gain by killing Binkie?"

Adam shrugged. They turned around and walked back to Seaview. Jenny barely slept a wink before it was time to get up and go to the café.

Brandon Newbury turned up at the Boardwalk Café for breakfast. Jenny was surprised when she saw him standing in line.

"Chocolate chip muffin?" she asked. "My treat."

"Can I talk to you?" Brandon pleaded.

Jenny led him out to the deck. A brisk wind whipped her hair against her face. She shivered a bit as she waited for Brandon to speak up.

"A cold front's coming in," Brandon began.

"Are you here to talk about the weather?" Jenny asked impatiently.

She had a mountain of work waiting for her in the kitchen.

"Did you hear about Binkie?" he asked.

Jenny nodded affirmatively.

"The police think I did it."

Jenny sat down at a table and motioned Brandon to do the same.

"What did you have against him?"

"He wasn't Kelly's cousin," Brandon explained. "He was her lover. The police think I wanted revenge."

"Did you?" Jenny asked simply.

Brandon ran a hand through his hair. His blue eyes looked troubled as he stared beseechingly at Jenny.

"I never had a clue," he said. "At least not at first. Binkie was so friendly. He was a guy's guy, you know. He was the only family Kelly had, or so I thought. Then I saw them together. I got the shock of my life."

"You had no idea?"

"I knew Kelly was up to something," Brandon admitted. "I thought maybe she was just having a last fling. But I never guessed she was carrying on with Binkie."

"Do you know what their plan was?" Jenny asked.

"My grandma told me," Brandon said. "I still can't believe it."

"Anyone in your position would feel cheated. You might have decided to get revenge."

"I couldn't stand the sight of him," Brandon admitted. "But I didn't do anything to hurt him. You have to believe me."

"Can you tell me anything about him?" Jenny asked. "What did he do in the city?"

"Binkie was between jobs," Brandon told Jenny. "As far as I know he didn't seem concerned about it."

Jenny didn't want to make any tall promises.

"Nothing about this business makes any sense," she told Brandon. "I'm not sure if I'll be able to help you."

"You are close to the sheriff, aren't you?" Brandon said. "At least put in a good word for me."

Jenny felt her temper flare.

"I don't interfere in Adam's work."

Brandon knew when to shut up. He implored Jenny to help him in any way she could. Jenny was relieved when he left.

The Magnolias came in for their daily ritual. None of them said anything much. The news of Binkie's death had spread through town. People were beginning to look worried. They huddled together and talked in soft voices, blaming the police for inaction.

Jenny was too distracted to cook anything elaborate for lunch. She made her strawberry chicken salad and added in some freshly picked basil for flavor. She packed a lunch basket and headed to the police station, hoping to get the latest scoop.

Adam greeted her with a scowl.

"Thanks for getting lunch," he said. "I'm sorry I won't be able to join you."

"I can go back to the café and eat on my own," Jenny said meekly. "Actually, I might look in on the baby. I need something to cheer me up."

Adam gave in, just as Jenny had expected.

"You can eat here," he said, rolling his eyes. "Just make sure you don't talk shop."

"We don't have to talk at all," Jenny said.

Adam ate half his sandwich in a couple of bites. Jenny took one dainty bite and chewed slowly. The phone on Adam's desk trilled, shattering the silence.

Adam picked up the receiver and listened. His face turned darker with every passing second. He slammed the phone down after a while and muttered something under his breath.

"Bad news?" Jenny asked sympathetically.

Adam stuffed the remaining sandwich in his mouth, refusing to answer Jenny. She could sense he was bursting to tell her something. He guzzled the lemonade Jenny had brought along and looked at her.

"A witness has come forward. Brandon Newbury was seen at the country club two nights ago."

"So he spent time at his club," Jenny shrugged. "No big deal."

"He was seen skulking around Binkie's room," Adam thundered.

"How do you know this witness is telling the truth?" Jenny demanded.

"It's my job to determine that," Adam said. "Lunch is over."

Jenny took the hint and picked up her basket. She walked back to the café, trying to guess who might have called the police against Brandon. Did someone in town have a grudge against him?

Ada Newbury was waiting for Jenny at the Boardwalk Café.

"Where have you been?" she complained. "I have been waiting for an hour."

"How can I help you, Mrs. Newbury?" Jenny asked, ignoring the old woman's outburst.

"My Brandon's in trouble," Ada sobbed. "That poor boy! Please say you will help him. I will pay you anything you want."

"It's not that easy," Jenny said, trying to be honest. "Nothing about this affair has made any sense."

"You know my Brandon works for a senator?" Ada asked. "He has big aspirations. Who was this Binkie? A good-for-nothing loafer. Why would my Brandon risk his life's work over someone like that?"

A tear rolled down Ada's rheumy eyes. Jenny felt sorry for her. She decided not to mention the witness.

"Calm down, Mrs. Newbury," she consoled. "If Brandon's innocent, he has nothing to worry about."

Jenny wasn't sure he was. Brandon had motive and opportunity and it was going to be difficult to prove he was completely free of blame.

# Chapter 17

Jenny smoothed her hands over her golf dress, gazing at herself in the mirror. She hoped it wasn't hopelessly out of fashion. She didn't want to look out of place.

Jenny needed an excuse to go scout around the country club. She had decided to take advantage of Zac Gordon's offer. She had called him the previous day and set up a lesson with him.

"Are you sure they will let me in?" she had joked.

Zac had boasted about the clout he wielded at the club.

"The golf course is my domain. Don't worry about a thing."

Two hours later, Jenny stood on the green, ready to tee off. Zac Gordon had painstakingly given her some directions, and attempted to correct her posture.

Jenny found out her game wasn't too rusty after all. She chatted with Zac as they traversed the famous course.

"This place is beautiful," Jenny breathed. "Do you like working here?"

"It's more than just a job," Zac told her. "I'm not

complaining. I get to do what I love most. And the tips aren't bad either."

Jenny spotted a familiar figure in the distance. She waved at the tall black haired youngster and called him over.

"What are you doing here?"

Enrique looked surprised to see her.

"I'm here to pick up my girlfriend. Her shift ends in a few minutes."

"Do you come here often?" Jenny asked.

Enrique shrugged.

"Pretty much, I guess."

Jenny turned to smile at Zac.

"You know Enrique, don't you?"

A look of annoyance flashed across Zac's face.

"Sure," he said. "The pool boy."

"Yes," Enrique grinned. "I'm the pool boy."

He said goodbye to Jenny and started walking away.

"You don't like him much, do you?" Jenny asked Zac.

"Is it that obvious?" Zac asked. "I told Ada, I mean Mrs. Newbury, she should fire him. He's a crook if I ever saw one."

"He's just a kid," Jenny said mildly. "He's a bit cocky, I guess."

"He's hanging around here all the time," Zac spat. "I saw him 2-3 nights ago, prowling around."

Jenny's mind connected the dots. That was the night Binkie had been killed. What had Enrique been doing at the country club?"

"Are you sure it was Enrique you saw?" Jenny asked Zac.

"I'm pretty sure," Zac nodded. "I had just finished a lesson and was going to the café to grab a drink. He came over to say Hi. Wanted to know if I could give him a free lesson sometime."

Jenny thought about Zac's words on her way back home. What could Enrique possibly have against Binkie? Binkie, on the other hand, could have had a grudge against Enrique for blackmailing Kelly. None of it made sense.

Jenny took a long hot shower, trying to relax. She decided to have a quiet evening at home, reading a book or watching some cooking show on TV. She had barely put her feet up when her phone rang. Heather and Molly were at the local pub for drinks. They wanted Jenny to join them.

Jenny pulled on a dressy top over her jeans and drove to the Rusty Anchor, Pelican Cove's favorite watering hole. Molly and Heather sat at a table, facing Chris and Jason.

"Where's the baby?" Jenny asked Jason as she greeted everyone.

"Betty Sue's watching her."

"We insisted Jason join us for a pint," Molly explained. "He hasn't had an evening to himself since the baby got here."

"I can spare thirty minutes," Jason said, glancing at his watch. "Then I'm gone."

"What's Adam doing tonight?" Chris asked Jenny.

"Working," Jenny said with a shrug.

"No he's not," Heather said, looking up.

Adam Hopkins had just entered the pub. He spotted Jenny and limped toward her, leaning on his cane.

"When are you two setting a wedding date?" Heather asked Adam.

"What is this, an ambush?" Adam asked grumpily.

He looked at Jenny.

"Did you put her up to this?"

"No, she didn't," Heather butted in. "I'm asking because I am getting too old to be a bridesmaid."

"No Heather, you're getting too old to be a bride," Adam smirked. "Why don't you take pity on your poor grandmother and find someone who will tolerate you for the rest of your life?"

Heather looked like she had been punched in the face. Jenny gave Adam a quelling look and went around the table to console her.

"What's the matter with you, Adam?" she cried.

"Sorry, long day," Adam apologized. "Don't mind me, Heather."

He stood up to leave.

"I should go."

He looked at Jenny.

"I need to take Tank out. We'll come to Seaview in a bit."

Jenny stopped at Mama Rosa's on her way home. She

picked up two large pizzas and salads for dinner. She drove home, telling herself to be patient with Adam.

Star was chatting with Adam when Jenny got home. Tank gave her his usual exuberant welcome. They devoured the food Jenny had brought and sat in the living room, eating bowls of chocolate ice cream.

Adam offered to call Heather and apologize again.

"It's your leg, isn't it?" Jenny asked. "Have you been doing those exercises the therapist recommended?"

"It's not just my leg," Adam sighed. "It's this case. It gets more complicated every day."

Jenny knew a direct question would not get her any answers. She stayed quiet.

"I did a background check on Paul Briggs," Adam said. "He just received a big sum of money in his bank account."

Jenny sat up, looking surprised.

"There have been multiple deposits into his account, all from different places in the area," Adam continued. "They add up to a pretty large amount."

"What does it mean?" Jenny asked.

"Looks like someone was paying him off," Adam said.

"But I don't understand why."

"The only people Binkie knew in town were Kelly and Brandon," Jenny said.

"Brandon Newbury is implicated again," Adam said, rubbing his eyes.

"How so?" Jenny asked.

"Binkie must have seen something. Say he named a price for his silence. Brandon paid him once but Binkie got greedy and asked for more. Brandon decided to silence him forever."

"That's just a theory," Jenny protested.

"It's a strong motive," Adam said seriously.

"Can you prove Brandon deposited the money in Binkie's account?"

"Not yet," Adam said, clenching his jaw. "The money was deposited in cash. It will take us some time to locate the person who made those payments."

"I'm sure you will get to the bottom of this soon," Jenny soothed.

They went for a walk on the beach after that. Adam and Tank left around ten, Adam feeling considerably better after stretching his legs.

Jenny spent a restless night, tossing and turning in bed. She had to prove Brandon's innocence, but she needed to believe in him herself before she did that.

A bright and sunny day dawned in Pelican Cove, putting a smile on Jenny's face. She hoped they had seen the last of the dark clouds. The citizens of Pelican Cove turned out to enjoy the fair weather. The Boardwalk Café was packed for breakfast, with some people waiting in line outside to get a table. Jenny stayed busy baking batches of muffins and making her special puttanesca omelets.

Once the breakfast rush receded, Jenny started a pot of tomato soup and cooked teriyaki chicken for lunch. The Magnolias arrived as usual, eager to talk about Jenny's day on the golf course.

"Can you handle the lunch crowd again?" Jenny asked her aunt. "Please?"

"Don't worry about the café," Star assured her. "But promise me you will be careful."

"I will," Jenny promised. "There's nothing to worry about. Heather's going with me."

"Where are we going?" Heather asked as the car sped over the bridge connecting Pelican Cove to the mainland.

Jenny brought her up to speed. Heather's eyes widened

as she heard about the money.

"What's the plan?" she asked Jenny.

"I have thought of something," Jenny said. "Not sure if it's going to work, though."

Jenny had shortlisted a few banks in neighboring towns. They entered the first one on her list and looked around. Jenny zeroed in on one young girl who seemed to be chatting freely with all the customers.

"Excuse me," Jenny said meekly, approaching her.

"How can I help you?" the girl asked.

Jenny hunched her shoulders and widened her eyes.

"I'm not sure you can. I'm getting married in a few weeks, see?"

The girl squealed and congratulated Jenny.

"We didn't register anywhere because we decided not to accept gifts. But you know how some people just have to send you something. Some of my friends and relatives put money in my account."

"How sweet!" the girl said sincerely.

"Yes," Jenny agreed. "But I have a problem. They deposited cash so I have no way of knowing who did it. I can't even write a thank you note."

The girl sympathized with Jenny.

"Can't you just guess?" she asked. "Must be someone who is close to you."

"I thought the same!" Jenny exclaimed. "I have some photos of my wedding shower. Can you take a look at them please?"

The girl hesitated for a second and then nodded. Jenny pulled out her phone and scrolled through photos of Brandon and Kelly's wedding shower. She had been clicking pictures of her food but she had managed to capture a lot of the guests in the process.

The girl looked at the pictures twice and shook her head.

"I'm sorry, but none of these people look familiar."

Jenny thanked her and stepped out of the bank with Heather.

"Now what?" Heather asked.

"Now we repeat the same thing at other banks in the area."

They hit pay dirt at the third bank they visited. One of the tellers, another young, bubbly woman pointed to a picture of Ada Newbury.

"She was here a few days ago. I remember because very few people make cash deposits."

Jenny thanked her and hurried out, her mind already churning with possibilities.

"What has Ada been up to?" Heather voiced as they got into the car. "Are you going to tell the police?"

"Not yet," Jenny answered. "I want to talk to Ada first."

"Won't Adam be mad at you for withholding information?"

"We don't know if a crime was committed."

"Why would Ada pay Binkie?" Heather asked. "I'm sure she barely tolerated him."

"You remember that argument Ada had with Kelly on the night of the party? She was offering to pay Kelly to leave Brandon."

"She didn't need to do that once Kelly was gone," Heather said patiently. "I think you are getting your timelines mixed up."

"You're right, Heather," Jenny said, slapping herself on the forehead. "What am I thinking?"

"Your brain needs food," Heather laughed. "I, for one, am starving. Let's look for some place to have lunch."

Jenny spotted an old, faded sign for a diner at the corner of a country lane. She yanked her wheel and turned on to the road, hoping the diner was open and still serving food. It turned out to be a gem of a find.

"What will you have?" an elderly woman with gray hair arranged in a neat bun asked them, pointing toward a chalkboard on the wall.

Jenny thought of Petunia, the previous owner of the Boardwalk Café. Jenny missed her every day.

Jenny chose the whitefish sandwich and Heather chose a grilled trout salad. Their meal came with crispy crinkle cut fries seasoned with Old Bay.

Jenny closed her eyes as she savored the fish, delicately flavored with dried herbs.

Heather dug her fork in her salad and took a big bite. Her eyes narrowed as she chewed the soft, flaky fish. She voiced the question that had been rolling around in Jenny's mind for the past hour.

"Do you think Ada's been playing you all along?"

# Chapter 18

Jenny dropped Heather off at the Bayview Inn. She headed into the hills toward the Newbury estate. Heather's question had riled her up. Jenny felt sure Ada Newbury had been lying to her. The more she thought about it, the angrier she got. Her face was flushed when she pulled up outside the massive iron gates. The security guard did his thing and let her through. Ten minutes later, she was jabbing her finger against the doorbell, trying to calm down.

A maid led her to the parlor. Ada was sitting on a sofa next to Zac Gordon, sipping tea and laughing at something he said. Her face fell when she saw Jenny.

"How many times have I told you to call before coming?" she snarled.

"We need to talk, Mrs. Newbury," Jenny said firmly.

"I'm busy at the moment," Ada said. "Why don't you wait out on the patio?"

She rang a small silver bell to summon the maid.

"This is important," Jenny stressed.

"I'm sure it can wait," Ada insisted.

"Ladies, ladies …" Zac Gordon interrupted. "Take it easy."

He urged Jenny to take a seat.

"How about some tea?" he asked.

Jenny couldn't wait to confront Ada but she didn't want to do it in Zac Gordon's presence.

"Actually, Zac, could you excuse us? I need a moment alone with Mrs. Newbury."

"No problem," Zac said, getting up.

The smile on his face was intact.

"I'll be outside. A stroll through the garden sounds perfect."

He patted Ada on the shoulder and left the room.

Jenny took a chair opposite Ada and settled down.

"What do you want?" Ada asked Jenny.

"Why did you put money in Binkie's account? Were you paying him off for something?"

"Who is this Binkie?" Ada wrinkled her nose in disgust.

"You know Binkie. Kelly's cousin. The guy they found

dead at the country club."

"You mean her lover?" Ada snorted. "I was right. Kelly was cheating on my Brandon. And she had the gall to bring that man to my party."

"All that is water under the bridge," Jenny dismissed. "I want to know if you made any payments into Binkie's account."

"Of course I did no such thing," Ada replied.

"You were seen at some banks in nearby towns. You made certain cash deposits. Do you still deny that?"

Ada had turned white. She didn't say anything for a few minutes. Jenny let her stew.

"The police will be on to you soon, Mrs. Newbury."

"I did make a deposit," Ada said hoarsely. "But it had nothing to do with Kelly's lover."

"Why should I believe you?" Jenny asked. "You have been keeping secrets from me since the beginning. You didn't tell me about your argument with Kelly. And now this!"

"I'm not lying about this," Ada pleaded.

"Couldn't you just write a check?" Jenny asked. "Why sneak off to a town fifty miles away and pay cash? Are you in some kind of trouble?"

"I can't talk about it. You'll just have to trust me on this."

"That's a tall order, Mrs. Newbury," Jenny sighed. "Someone's been depositing money into Binkie's account. The police are trying to find this person. It won't be long before they identify you."

"Do you think they will arrest me?"

Jenny didn't have an answer for that.

"They will suspect you again at the very least."

"I can tell you when I made the deposits," Ada said hesitantly. "And the amount I paid. But I can't tell you who I gave the money to."

"That might help," Jenny said.

She had a strong suspicion about who the recipient of Ada's largesse was. She was ready to bet he was strolling in the garden outside.

Zac Gordon peeped in at a window just then.

"Are you two done?" he asked. "The wind's a bit harsh out here."

"Come on in," Ada said.

Zac ambled in and sat on the sofa again. Jenny noticed he wasn't dressed for golf. The jeans and shirt he wore indicated he was off duty.

"I enjoyed my golf lesson the other day," Jenny said to Zac. "You are a really good coach."

"You are a good player," Zac offered. "Spend an hour with me every day and you will be ready to go pro."

"I don't have time for that," Jenny smiled. "I have a café to run."

"And some sleuthing to do on the side, huh?" Zac asked.

His eyes hardened for a second and then he was his genial self again.

"Ada tells me you like to snoop around."

"I just talk to people," Jenny said modestly.

"It's time for our golf lesson," Ada said to Zac.

She gave Jenny a pointed look.

"Didn't you have a stiff neck?" Zac asked Ada.

"I'm leaving anyway," Jenny said, getting up.

Jenny stepped out into the hallway outside the parlor and looked around. She urgently needed to use a restroom. A couple of passages forked off in different directions making Jenny hesitate. She had used a powder room at the Newbury mansion before but Heather had guided her to it.

Jenny walked down a bunch of closed doors, trying to remember the right one. Every door looked the same. She paused in front of one tentatively and sucked in a breath. She knocked twice just in case and pushed the door in, walking in on a couple locked in a tight embrace.

"I'm sorry," Jenny began.

Then her eyes widened in shock.

"Brandon! I'm sorry, I didn't realize this was your room."

"It's not," Brandon said cheerfully. "It's a guest room. It's unoccupied at present. Were you looking to use the powder room?"

Jenny nodded mutely.

The girl next to Brandon had straightened up a bit.

"How are you?" she greeted Jenny.

"I'm good, Megan. How are you?" Jenny said mechanically.

She rushed to the door Brandon pointed at. Brandon was alone in the room when she came out five minutes later.

"Megan had to leave," he said.

"So …" Jenny said. "You and Megan, huh?"

"We never really stopped loving each other," Brandon clarified.

"But I thought she was the one who dumped you."

"It was all a big misunderstanding," Brandon said with a frown. "Megan thought I was interested in someone else. She didn't want to be a burden. So she took the initiative and let me go."

"But you were still in love with her," Jenny prompted.

"That's right," Brandon said proudly. "Megan and I have been friends for years. She is my first love."

"Are you two engaged?"

"We are going to wait for a few weeks before we announce our engagement," Brandon said soberly. "I might just tell my grandma. She adores Megan."

"Congratulations," Jenny said warmly. "I hope you will be happy together." She wavered a bit before asking her next question. "Tell me one thing. Were you really going to marry Kelly?"

"Frankly, I don't know. I feel like such a fool now. She had me wound around her finger. I never realized she was just using me."

Jenny wondered when Brandon had realized that. Had he confronted Kelly on the night of the party?

The sky had darkened by the time Jenny said goodbye to Brandon and stepped out. The orange ball of the sun had almost set, painting the sky around it in shades of pink and tangerine.

Jenny yawned deeply and started her car. Multiple theories were churning in her mind but she didn't have the energy to process any of them. All she wanted to do was go home and soak in a hot bath. Jenny's eyes glazed over as she thought of lighting a bunch of scented candles and using the lavender bath salts her aunt had got for her.

Suddenly, a pair of bright headlights appeared in her rearview mirror, almost blinding her. The portion of road Jenny was on was on the outskirts of town. There was hardly any traffic on the road. Jenny changed the lane and veered to the right, allowing the car behind her to pass. The headlights stayed behind her.

Jenny realized they were too close. Her car was almost on the shoulder now. She guessed the vehicle behind her was some kind of big truck. Jenny put on her turn signal and pulled her car completely on the shoulder. Surely the other car would pass her once she came to a stop?

Jenny felt her car skid as the car behind her rammed into her. Jenny spun her wheel round and round, trying to remember what she was supposed to do in this kind of situation. Her car tipped over and plunged into a ditch, with one wheel spinning in the air.

The car behind her flashed its lights and sped off.

Jenny wriggled in her seat, trying to reach her bag. Then she remembered her cell phone was in the cup holder right next to her. Finally, she dialed the emergency number with trembling fingers and waited for help.

Adam arrived on the scene within minutes, along with the ambulance. He stood by impatiently while Jenny was pulled out of the car. The paramedics treated her for a few bruises and recommended she go to the hospital to get checked out.

Three hours later, Jenny was tucked in her bed with a bowl of hot chicken soup. Her aunt sat next to her and Adam paced the room, his face as black as thunder.

"You could have been hurt, really hurt," he said hoarsely.

Jenny's hand shook as she spooned some soup into

her mouth. She knew Adam was right. So she let him rave at her.

"There's a lot of maniacs out there," Star said. "Jenny was in the wrong place at the wrong time."

"I don't agree," Adam said heavily.

Jenny had been briefly questioned by the police. They had wanted to get a description of the car or driver. Jenny hadn't had a glimpse of either. All she could say was it was a big truck, much bigger than her small sedan.

Jenny had told them how the car had followed her for a long time and rammed into her a couple of times. She agreed it had seemed like a deliberate move and not an accident.

"How do you always get into these scrapes?" Adam asked hoarsely. "Why can't you stay out of trouble for once?"

"Take it easy, son." Star's voice had a warning note in it.

"Why would someone want to hurt me?" Jenny asked.

"You have made someone feel threatened," Adam said. "You must be getting close."

"If I am, I don't know it."

"What have you been doing in the past two days?" Adam wanted to know.

Jenny gave him a brief account of where she had been.

"So Brandon Newbury knew you were going to be on that road," Adam said. "I don't trust that guy one bit."

"Brandon, really?" Jenny asked. "Well, if you want to put it that way, everyone at the Newbury estate knew I was going to drive back to town. Ada knew, so did her entire staff."

"You need to take it easy for a while," Adam said. "Promise me you won't leave the house."

"That's impossible," Jenny exploded. "What about the café"?"

"We can take care of the café," Star said. "Don't worry about it."

"I'm not going to be cooped up in here just because some coward tried to run me off the road."

"My men are working on this now," Adam said, pausing next to Jenny's bed. "At least give them a couple of days."

"The doctor advised you to rest," Star reminded her. "Why don't you take this opportunity and relax a bit?"

"One day!" Jenny said, holding up a finger. "I will stay home for one day. Then I am going back to the café."

"And you will stop trying to solve this case?" Adam asked hopefully.

Jenny stirred her soup and smiled wanly at Adam. She didn't make promises she couldn't keep.

# Chapter 19

Star knocked on Jenny's door the next morning and entered bearing a loaded tray.

Jenny reclined against a mound of pillows, reading a book.

"Good Morning," Star greeted her. "I hope you are hungry."

Jenny stared at the stack of blueberry pancakes, bacon, eggs and toast. A dewy pink rose from the garden rested on the tray.

"Breakfast in bed?" Jenny exclaimed, staring at the food in fascination. "What am I, an invalid?"

"I'm allowed to spoil my niece a bit," Star pouted.

She sat down at the edge of the bed and gave Jenny a worried look.

"I have loved having you here with me," she said.

"I'm not going anywhere," Jenny soothed. "Now let's eat this delicious breakfast you have cooked for me."

Jenny forced her aunt to eat along with her. There was plenty of food for the both of them.

"I need to get going," Star said. "Heather must be waiting for me."

Heather had volunteered to open the Boardwalk Café that morning and get breakfast started.

"Thank her for me, will you?" Jenny said. "Tell her I owe her one."

"You can tell her yourself," Star said with a smile. "We look out for each other in this town."

There was another knock on the door and Jason Stone entered. The baby was strapped to his body in a sling like carrier.

Jenny's face lit up when she saw Jason.

"This is a surprise!" she cried, holding out her arms toward Emily. "Give me that darling."

Jason gently pulled Emily out and handed her over to Jenny. Jenny kissed the baby's forehead and cuddled her. The baby gurgled and pulled a lock of Jenny's hair.

"We heard about your little mishap," Jason said. "What's the damage?"

"I'm perfectly alright," Jenny said. "My car, on the other hand, needs some care."

"Carry on, you two," Star said.

Jenny had completely forgotten her aunt.

"Will you keep an eye on her?" Star asked Jason. "I have to go to the café."

"Emily and I will stand guard," Jason said with a smile. "Don't worry about a thing, Star."

"Are you guys in collusion?" Jenny asked after Star had stepped out. "I would be very cross, except, you brought this little bundle of joy. Emily and I are going to have a fine visit."

Jenny chatted with Jason for a while. Jason brought in his bag after some time and pulled out some files.

"I hope you don't mind?" he apologized to Jenny. "I need to get this done by evening."

Emily took a nap after a while. Jenny went down to the kitchen and hunted around in her freezer for a casserole for lunch. She found a pan of Star's famous six layer lasagna and slid it into the oven.

"You must be getting close," Jason said as he prepared Emily's bottle. "You are beginning to threaten someone."

"I have no idea who," Jenny sighed. "It's all like a really intricate web. And there's something in the water, Jason. Every person I meet seems to be having an affair."

"You drank a bit of that water yourself," Jason teased.

"That's different," Jenny argued. "Adam and I are in love."

Jason's eyelids flickered a bit and he squared his shoulders but Jenny didn't notice any of that.

"I'm talking about a proper affair, the kind you have when you are cheating on someone."

"Oh?" Jason asked with interest.

Jenny started counting off her fingers.

"Kelly was having an affair with Binkie, she was sweet on the pool boy too. Ada is having a fling with the golf pro at her club …"

"Wait a minute," Jason interrupted. "What?"

"Have you met the golf pro at the country club?"

Jenny knew Jason was a member and enjoyed a good round of golf. It was all part of being a successful lawyer.

"I haven't been on the links in a while," Jason explained. "I was too busy earlier and now with Emily, it's out of the question."

"Zac Gordon is tall and attractive, and he says all the

right things."

"Surely he's younger than Ada?" Jason sputtered.

"By decades," Jenny nodded. "They were seen smooching in a deserted alley."

"Now I've heard it all," Jason sniggered.

"Not really," Jenny said. "Brandon's back with Megan."

"They have been in love since they were kids," Jason told Jenny. "I was shocked to learn Brandon was marrying someone else."

"What if Brandon got back with Megan while Kelly was still alive?" Jenny asked. "He knew she was cheating on him. How do we know he didn't do the same?"

"He would have been justified," Jason said.

"I don't know about that," Jenny said. "But having an affair with Megan gives him a motive."

They went back and forth over it for a while.

"Are you sure about Ada? I can't imagine Ada Newbury being friendly with someone of the working class."

Emily woke up with a cry and Jason hastened to feed her. By the time Jenny set the table and served the lasagna, Emily's eyelids were drooping again.

Father and daughter left after lunch, Jason urging Jenny to take better care of herself.

Jenny had barely had time to flip through the latest issue of her favorite cooking magazine when she heard some familiar voices outside. She sprang up and flung the door open, just as Heather raised her hand to knock.

"What are you all doing here?" Jenny beamed. "This is a pleasant surprise."

Betty Sue, Heather and Molly bustled in, followed by Star. Star gave Jenny a withering look.

"You were supposed to take it easy, take a nap or something."

"I'm fine," Jenny assured her. "You worry too much."

She pointed to the container Molly held in her hands.

"Dessert?"

"You bet," Molly said. "My special espresso brownies."

Betty Sue settled in a comfortable armchair and pulled out her knitting. Her needles clacked in a familiar rhythm as she spoke to Jenny.

"We decided you needed our help. This whole sordid business has gone on too long."

"What did you have in mind?" Jenny asked, taking a big bite of Molly's gooey, rich brownie.

She hadn't waited for Molly to serve them on a plate. Molly handed the plate around and nodded at Betty Sue.

"We know you're the real sleuth, Jenny, but maybe if we brainstorm together, we might see something you have missed."

"Five heads are better than one," Jenny agreed.

"Where should we start?" Heather asked eagerly. "Enrique?"

"Heather told me that pool boy was blackmailing the poor girl who died," Betty Sue said. "Why would he kill her? He had lots to gain from her. And he seems to be the greedy type."

"That's right," Jenny said. "But he also has a criminal past. He was forcing Kelly to pay him for his silence. Let's not forget he was right there at the pool house. He could have let Kelly in."

"You think they had an argument?" Molly asked.

"They might have been fighting over money," Jenny agreed. "He could have pushed her in accidentally."

"What about the bruise on her head?" Heather asked. "I don't see Enrique hitting her on purpose."

"I agree," Jenny said. "But I'm not ready to rule him out completely."

"Okay," Molly said. "I think we are all in agreement on that one. Who else?"

"Brandon," Jenny said, looking at Heather. "I know you are related but we are trying to be objective here."

"It's okay," Heather said. "Let's get this out of the way."

"Brandon knew that girl was cheating on him, didn't he?" Betty Sue asked.

Jenny told the Magnolias about Megan and Brandon.

"I'm beginning to think he was cheating on Kelly too."

This was news to the other women. They exclaimed over this new theory, amazed at why the young couple had been going ahead with their wedding. Neither of them seemed interested in each other.

"Brandon may have wanted to break it off with Kelly," Jenny mused. "But Kelly wanted the wedding to happen. That was the whole point of the plan she hatched with Binkie. She wanted to trap Brandon in marriage and then maybe get a big divorce settlement."

"How does all this implicate Brandon?" Heather asked.

"Brandon decided to confront Kelly. He could have let her into the pool house. Maybe that was their rendezvous point."

"And then things got out of hand?" Molly asked. "That's possible. What about Binkie though? Why would Brandon kill him too?"

"Binkie was always hanging around Kelly," Jenny said. "Remember the night of the party? Those two were literally joined at the hip. Binkie could have followed Kelly to the pool house. He might have seen what Brandon did."

"And then he blackmailed Brandon?" Star spoke up. "There's a lot of that going around too."

"So what? Brandon got Binkie out of the way too?" Heather scoffed. "I can see Brandon losing his temper once but killing someone in cold blood, that's just not him."

"I understand your feelings, Heather," Jenny said. "But the evidence points toward him. He wasn't in bed when Kelly died, and he was at the country club around the time Binkie died. Like it or not, Brandon is the top suspect."

"What about that boy Binkie?" Betty Sue asked.

"That's right," Star spoke up. "He was a crook from what I can tell."

"There is one possible scenario," Jenny said. "Kelly might have changed her mind about ditching Brandon. She must have realized how rich the Newburys really were. What if she wanted to marry Brandon for real? That would leave Binkie in the lurch."

"And make him really angry with Kelly," Molly breathed, licking her chocolate stained fingers.

"Binkie could have argued with Kelly," Heather said, her eyes shining with hope. "Isn't it possible he hit her in a fit of anger?"

"There is only one problem with that theory," Jenny sighed. "Who killed Binkie?"

"That's it?" Star asked. "Are we out of suspects?"

"There's one other person who hated Kelly," Molly said.

"You are thinking of Ada," Betty Sue snorted. "Ada Newbury hates pretty much everyone other than her immediate family. If she started killing everyone she had an objection to, there would be a bloodbath in

Pelican Cove."

"Funny how you always take her side," Star quipped.

The two older women squabbled for some time.

"Give it a rest, you two," Jenny said.

She stood up and began pacing the room. The shadows were beginning to lengthen outside. The sheer white curtains at the windows flapped around in the breeze coming off the ocean. The day had turned cooler, making Jenny shiver all of a sudden.

"Are we missing something?" she spoke out loud. "Or someone?"

"There is the staff at the Newbury mansion," Heather said. "I don't care how many times they change the access code for that pool house, some of them must have known what it was."

"Why would they have a grudge against Kelly though? I don't think any of the staff has a clear motive. It just doesn't make sense."

"What about the people at the party?" Molly asked. "Maybe Kelly pulled the same racket on someone else before. This person could have followed her to Pelican Cove."

"It was a very exclusive gathering," Heather said. "You

know how snobbish Ada is. She went over the guest list with a fine toothcomb. Anyway, the party was for her friends, not Kelly's."

"We are back where we started," Jenny groaned. "Looks like whoever it was escaped long ago."

"That's not true," Star spoke up. "You must be getting close, Jenny. That's why someone tried to hurt you."

Heather and Molly bobbed their heads in agreement. Betty Sue summed up what they were all thinking.

"Whoever it is, he or she is watching every move you make, Jenny."

# Chapter 20

"I still can't believe Ada invited me today," Jenny said, tapping her hands on the steering wheel.

Jenny had become familiar with the winding road that led into the hills and the Newbury estate.

"She's warming up to you, Jenny." Heather laughed shrilly and teased her friend. "Ada Newbury is giving you time of day. Count your blessings."

She sniggered again, shaking her head.

"That's enough," Betty Sue Morse said from the back seat. "Make sure you behave yourself when we get there."

"Yes, Grandma!" Heather said with a roll of her eyes.

"What's the occasion?" Jenny looked into the rearview mirror and caught Betty Sue's eye.

"Brandon said it's a surprise," Heather spoke up before Betty Sue had a chance to respond.

"We'll find out soon enough," Betty Sue nodded. "Why are you so impatient?"

"I just hope I am dressed appropriately," Jenny said

self-consciously.

She was wearing a figure hugging silk dress in a light peach color. It was from an expensive label and she had worn it several times over the years. She hoped it was fancy enough for whatever event Ada had invited them to.

"You look fine," Heather reassured her friend.

"Is that fella of hers going to be there?" Betty Sue asked. "Maybe I can get a good look at him this time."

Ada had been spotted with Zac Gordon again. Star had come upon them when she was walking on the bluffs, trying to look for a good spot to set up her easel. Molly had seen them driving out of town once. The Magnolias had concluded that Ada Newbury was definitely involved in some way with the golf pro. Whether it was a light flirtation, an amorous affair or just an innocent friendship, they had no idea. The younger women were willing to bet that it was a hot affair. Especially since Ada's husband Julius had been away on business for the past few months.

"She wouldn't dare!" Heather exclaimed. "You think Brandon knows what Ada has been up to?"

"Brandon has been keeping himself busy," Jenny reminded her.

Brandon and Megan had been hanging out together for

the past few weeks. There was nothing hidden about their relationship.

Heather's face assumed an 'I told you so' expression.

"Brandon and Megan are meant for each other," she parroted.

Jenny pulled up at the Newbury's entrance and the security guard waved her in through the big iron gates.

A maid took their wraps and ushered them out to the garden at the back. Fairy lights glittered in the dusk, covering the extensive veranda. Paper lanterns were interspersed between them and hung on trees, bathing the surroundings in a soft glow. Jenny had a déjà vu moment as she thought of the night of Kelly's party.

Brandon rushed forward to greet them. Jenny saw Ada holding court over a small group of people. Megan sat next to Ada on a sofa. Zac Gordon reclined in an armchair.

Brandon showed them to their seats, making sure they were comfortable.

Greetings were exchanged. Betty Sue sat with her back ramrod straight. She gave Zac Gordon a withering look.

"I don't believe we have met before," she said loudly.

Zac Gordon opened his mouth to speak. Ada beat him to it.

"Zac is a close friend, Betty Sue."

Betty Sue's cheeks turned pink.

"Friend, huh?" she murmured. "Nice to meet you, Zac."

Brandon offered the ladies a drink.

"We are all having champagne. Will that do? I can get you a soda or tea if you like."

They chose champagne and Brandon poured some bubbly into flutes. Jenny noticed he had another glass beside him filled with a dark, amber liquid.

"Are we all here?" Heather asked. "Or is anyone else coming?"

"It's a small group," Ada said. "Just people I care about."

"What's the occasion?" Heather asked again. "Are we celebrating something?"

Brandon took Megan's hand in his. They looked at each other and beamed at the assembled group.

"We wanted you to be the first to know," Brandon

began. "Megan and I are engaged."

Heather squealed in delight. She stood up and gave Brandon a tight hug. Then she turned around and hugged Megan.

"I knew it!" she exclaimed. "You two are meant to be together."

Megan blushed like a new bride.

"Congratulations, you two," Jenny said, raising her champagne flute toward them. "Aren't you having a proper engagement?"

"We feel it's too soon," Brandon said. "You know, after Kelly ..."

Megan put a hand on his shoulder.

"We'll have a long engagement and then have a lavish wedding next year. Right, Mrs. Newbury?"

She turned toward Ada, seeking her approval.

"That's right, dear," Ada said. "And how many times have I told you? Call me Grandma, like Brandon does."

"Okay, Grandma Ada," Megan said shyly.

Jenny felt she was seeing a new version of Megan.

"Do you approve of this one then, Ada?" Betty Sue asked from her perch. "She may be local but she's not a Pioneer."

The five oldest families in Pelican Cove were called the Pioneers. They considered themselves superior to the rest and generally married among themselves.

"The Pattersons have lived in Pelican Cove for many generations," Ada said. "That's good enough for me."

"Are you sure about that, Grandma?" Brandon asked.

His voice was a bit slurred. Jenny decided he had imbibed a bit too much of hard liquor.

"Of course, dear," Ada said sharply. "Whatever do you mean?"

"Make sure she likes you, Megan," Brandon said, shaking Megan by the shoulder. "Or you'll be gone. Just like Kelly."

Megan looked weary. She picked up a tray of stuffed olives and offered them to Brandon.

"Why don't you eat something, sweetie?"

Brandon swept her hand aside.

"Grandma will make you go away. Look what happened to Kelly. She made her go away."

Megan's eyes darted between Ada and Brandon. She stood up and began to coax Brandon to his feet.

"Let's go get some solid food," she urged. "That whiskey's gone straight to your head."

"I'm not drunk, Megs," Brandon said, swaying on his feet.

He threw back his head and laughed. Then he pointed a shaky finger at Ada.

"You think I don't know what you did? You made Kelly go away. You, you witch…"

Ada's face turned white first, then red spots appeared on her cheeks.

"Take him inside, Megan," she said sternly. "Let him sleep it off."

"I'm not a child," Brandon cried suddenly. "And I'm not helpless like Kelly. You can't kill me off, you witch!"

Before Ada could respond to this latest insult, Zac Gordon shot out of his chair and lunged toward Brandon. His fist flew and caught Brandon on the jaw. Jenny heard a crack as the next punch broke Brandon's nose. He flailed his arms and crashed to the floor.

"Stop it!" Ada cried. "Stop fighting at once."

Megan had pulled out her phone and called the police.

Jenny and Heather huddled together and watched as Zac sat on Brandon's chest, continuing to pummel him. Betty Sue had obliged everyone by fainting on the spot.

Jenny finally spurred Heather and Megan into action. Together, they grabbed Zac by the arms and the collar of his shirt and tried to drag him away.

Ten minutes later, sirens sounded outside and the police rushed into the garden. Adam hobbled up to Jenny, his eyes full of concern.

"What just happened here?"

Brandon was sitting in a chair, holding a linen napkin against his nose. The girls had torn off Zac's sleeve and he sat opposite Brandon, shooting daggers at him. Ada was sobbing openly and Betty Sue fanned herself, muttering a prayer.

Jenny, Megan and Heather started talking at once. Adam held up his hand and asked Jenny to go on. Jenny gave him a precise account of how Zac had beaten Brandon to a pulp.

"We are taking you in," Adam told Zac.

He turned toward Brandon.

"I assume you want to press charges?"

"Of course I do," Brandon roared.

Ada opened her mouth to protest, but said nothing.

The police left the house with Zac in handcuffs.

Jenny caught Heather's eye and nodded at her. Heather helped Betty Sue to her feet and they started to leave.

"You really think I had something to do with that girl's death?" Ada asked Brandon. "How could you?"

Brandon looked uncomfortable.

"I'm sorry, Grandma!" he said. "I don't know what came over me."

Megan stood close to him, stroking his back.

"I really love Megan, Grandma," Brandon pleaded. "I always have. I couldn't take it if anything happened to her."

"I like her too," Ada said, bewildered. "She's been in an out of this house since she was a child. Your Grandpa and I always figured she would marry you one day."

Brandon sat down next to Ada. He looked like a lost child.

"I'm afraid, Grandma. Until we find out what happened to Kelly, I'll never feel safe. I know I didn't do it. And Binkie's dead. So who did it?"

Jenny, Heather and Betty Sue quietly said goodbye to Megan and walked out. Betty Sue sat wheezing in the back seat on the drive home. All the excitement had been too much for her. Heather couldn't stop talking.

Jenny was thoughtful, trying to process the scene she had witnessed. She felt she was on to something but she couldn't quite put her finger on it.

"What made Zac flip like that?" she asked Heather.

"Flip?" Heather laughed. "He went mental!"

Betty Sue spoke up from the back seat.

"Brandon called Ada a witch. That's what set off that young man."

"So Zac couldn't tolerate hearing anything bad against Ada," Jenny spoke out loud.

"He might have killed Brandon if we hadn't pulled him off," Heather crowed.

Jenny felt the pieces of the puzzle fall in place. Apparently, Zac Gordon could do anything for Ada. Had she hired him to get Kelly out of the way? She thought of Ada Newbury, an imposing old shrew.

How could a snob like Ada have a romantic relationship with a common golf pro? Maybe she had paid him to do her dirty work and he was forcing her now. Hanging out with Zac Gordon might be something Ada was doing under duress.

Jenny pulled the car onto the shoulder and came to a stop. She turned around in her seat and looked at Heather and Betty Sue, her eyes gleaming.

"Remember how we talked about who could have killed Kelly? We thought it had to be Brandon or Enrique. But there's one person we haven't considered all this time. Someone who was right in front of us."

"Zac Gordon?" Heather cried.

Jenny nodded.

"You just saw what happened. Zac seems to be Ada's personal watchdog."

"So Ada paid him to get Kelly out of the way?" Heather echoed Jenny's thoughts.

"I don't believe it," Betty Sue protested. "Ada would never do that."

"Ada may not have been specific," Jenny reasoned. "Maybe Zac went a bit overboard."

"Things got out of hand," Heather agreed. "And Kelly

lost her life. But what about Binkie?"

"I haven't figured that out yet," Jenny admitted. "Binkie might have seen something and Zac had to get rid of him."

"I think Ada is innocent," Betty Sue argued. "That boy must have acted on his own."

"But why?" Jenny and Heather chorused.

"To impress Ada?" Heather mused.

"Or try to please her?" Jenny added.

"Are we going to stay here all night talking about this?" Betty Sue demanded. "Take me home now."

Jenny started the car with a sigh. She needed to talk to Adam immediately. He would decide if he wanted to bring Ada Newbury in for further questioning.

# Chapter 21

Jenny wiped down a table at the Boardwalk Café, deep in thought. The breakfast rush had just ended. Jenny had started making her parfaits in a smaller serving size. Most people ordered them as a side or dessert to go with their hearty breakfast. Jenny's customers, both locals and tourists, wanted sumptuous fare like omelets and frittatas for their first meal of the day. She had learnt it the hard way and accepted that she didn't cater to a yogurt and granola type of crowd.

"Why don't you come into the kitchen and grab a bite?" Star said to her.

Jenny took a last look around the room, made sure everyone's coffee was topped up and went into the kitchen with her aunt. She picked up a spoon and began eating the special parfait of the day, strawberries with toasted coconut and hazelnuts.

The phone mounted on the kitchen wall trilled. Jenny set her food down and sprang up.

"Heather! Is everything okay?"

She nodded her head and listened quietly for a while before hanging up.

"Aren't they coming over today?" Star asked.

"The police just took Ada in for questioning," Jenny told her. "Brandon called Heather. He's going to pick up Jason and go to the police station."

"Wonder who's watching Emily," Star said. "Why don't you call Jason? We can take her for some time."

Jenny's cell phone rang just then. It was Jason, in dire need of a baby sitter. Jenny told him to drop the baby off at the café.

"We knew this was coming," Star said, referring to Heather's phone call.

"You think Ada will break down and confess?"

"Betty Sue is sure she is innocent," Star reminded Jenny. "But you think Ada is hiding something, don't you?"

"You know how finicky she is about status and bloodlines and all that crap," Jenny said. "And she really hated Kelly."

"Let's see what Adam finds out."

The Magnolias came in at ten and took turns singing and talking to the baby. Heather offered to take her back to the Bayview Inn.

"Call that young man of yours," Betty Sue told Jenny. "Find out what's happening with Ada."

"You know he doesn't like to be disturbed, Betty Sue. I'll let you know as soon as I find out anything."

The Magnolias dispersed soon after. Heather was eager to go back to the inn with Emily. She had pulled her old crib out of the attic and set it up in a corner of their living room. She was eager to see how the baby liked it.

Adam came to the Boardwalk Café around noon, making Jenny's eyes widen in surprise.

"Got something to eat?" he asked Jenny. "I had to skip breakfast. I'm starving."

Jenny set a big bowl of mushroom soup before Adam and told him to get started. She brought out a couple of buffalo chicken sandwiches and sat down before him.

"Ada insists she is innocent and I am inclined to believe her," he said, between spoonfuls of soup.

Jenny was surprised Adam was willingly sharing information with her but she wasn't going to stare a gift horse in the mouth.

"So she didn't hire Zac Gordon to do her dirty work," Jenny asked, her mouth drooping in disappointment.

"She says she didn't and there is no evidence to prove otherwise."

"What about her relationship with Zac?" Jenny shot back. "Did she deny that too?"

Adam bit into his sandwich and chewed appreciatively.

"This is like chicken wings dipped in blue cheese with a side of celery," he said. "Yum!"

Jenny wasn't interested in Adam's compliments.

"Adam!"

"Ada was very forthcoming about it," Adam said with a smile. "She is having a fling with the golf pro."

"But why?" Jenny cried. "He has to be at least thirty years younger than her."

"Is that your only objection?" Adam quirked an eyebrow.

"She's married, of course," Jenny added. "How could she cheat on Julius?"

"Ada doesn't feel the need to explain herself," Adam said.

"Did she ask you to release Zac Gordon?" Jenny asked.

Adam shook his head.

"Blood is thicker than water. She was shocked by how

he behaved. She said she wasn't aware he had a violent side. He's been all lovey-dovey with her, obviously. She is going to insist that Brandon press charges against Zac. She wants us to put him away forever."

"That's quite an about turn," Jenny laughed.

"She's nothing if not whimsical," Adam said.

"What do you think about this whole business?" Jenny asked. "Do you think Zac could have done it?"

"We never considered Zac as a suspect before," Adam said. "Now we are looking into his alibi for both the murders. And I'm doing a background check on him too."

Adam coaxed Jenny into sharing a sandwich with him. He left soon after.

A few more customers wandered in for a late lunch. The café emptied after that. Star and Jenny did a quick job of cleaning up and went into the kitchen to prep for the next day.

They were almost ready to leave when Jenny heard someone out on the deck.

A young man stood outside, biting his nails.

"Enrique!" Jenny exclaimed. "What are you doing here?"

"Can we talk?" he asked hesitantly.

"Sure," Jenny said, pointing to a chair. "What's on your mind?"

"Can you keep this between us?" Enrique asked. "I need to be sure you won't turn me in."

Jenny looked alarmed.

"What have you done? I can't promise anything."

Enrique's brow pinched as he wavered for a minute. Then he let out a deep sigh and started talking.

Jenny's eyes grew larger as she listened to Enrique's story. Her mouth dropped open after a while. She almost jogged to the police station to bring Adam up to speed on Enrique's story.

Things happened rapidly after that. Adam told Jenny about it when they were having dinner two days later.

Zac Gordon confessed to the murder of both Kelly and Binkie. The first murder had happened at the pool house and Enrique witnessed it when he woke up and went to the kitchen for a drink of water. He had watched Zac bash Kelly in the head with a golf club and push her into the pool. He had rushed to help Kelly as soon as Zac left the scene. It had been too late to save Kelly. Afraid of being harassed by the police, he went in and pretended he had been asleep in the pool house all night. Then he got greedy and tried to blackmail Zac.

Zac Gordon had threatened to report Enrique to immigration. It had been a shot in the dark but it had found its mark. It turned out Enrique was undocumented. Faced with the threat of being deported, he didn't say a word against Zac.

"What about Binkie?" Jenny asked Adam.

She was still trying to wrap her head around all the facts. It seemed Zac, Enrique and Binkie had all been crooks, using blackmail to extract money from someone.

"Binkie spotted Ada and Zac together," Adam smirked. "He threatened to expose their little affair. Zac thought that would be a big embarrassment for Ada, so he paid up at first. Then Binkie's demands increased. So Zac got him out of the way."

"I always thought Zac was a player, I mean, a womanizer," Jenny said, "but I never took him for a cold blooded killer."

"He had a violent past," Adam reported. "He beat up a few people when he was on the golf circuit, apparently for no reason at all. If he hadn't injured his shoulder and left himself, he would have been banned from the game."

"I don't understand one thing," Jenny said, taking a sip of her wine. "What was his motive? Why did he murder Kelly?"

"He did it for Ada," Adam said.

"What?" Jenny exclaimed.

"You know Ada can be outspoken. She made it very clear that she didn't like Kelly. She didn't want Brandon to marry her."

"There were other ways to break them up."

"He saw Ada trying to bribe Kelly into leaving Brandon. He asked her to meet him by the pool and threatened her. She scoffed at him. That's when he attacked her. He thought it would make Ada happy."

"I guess it did, in a way," Jenny mused. "What does Ada say about all this? Did she know what Zac was up to?"

"She's in shock. She had no idea what was going on in Zac's mind. She kept repeating it over and over again. I believe her."

"How did those two get together anyway?" Jenny asked, thinking she hadn't come across a more unlikely alliance in a long time.

"Zac flirts around with women his age," Adam said.

"Mostly women at the country club. I guess he used to mooch off them. He never expected to fall for Ada."

"Was it mutual?" Jenny asked.

"Both of them say it was. Ada decided to learn golf while Julius was away on his extended trip. She wanted to surprise him when he got back. She met Zac at the club and they became friends. You know the rest."

"What happens to Enrique?" Jenny asked. "Will they send him back?"

"Enrique is working with an immigration lawyer. Brandon recommended one. I think he's going to be fine."

"Two young people lost their life, all for nothing," Jenny said sadly.

"Don't forget Kelly and Binkie were out to dupe Brandon. They might have met with trouble sooner or later."

"Brandon's back with his first love now," Jenny smiled. "He's happy with Megan."

Adam took Jenny's hand in hers and gazed deeply into her eyes.

"What about us, Jenny? Do you think it's time?"

# Epilogue

The spring sun bathed Pelican Cove in a bright glow.
Flowers bloomed everywhere and lawns were carpeted
in newly sprouted grass in rich emerald hues. A
barbecue was in progress on Jenny's patio, amidst a
vibrant garden heavy with the scent of roses and
gardenias.

Jason and Chris stood at a large grill, roasting hot dogs
and flipping burgers. The Magnolias sat a short
distance away, sipping tall glasses of cool lemonade,
playing with the baby. Emily sat in her stroller, her big,
round eyes taking everything in. She clapped her hands
and cooed at the women, speaking in her own special
baby language.

"Where is that young man of yours?" Betty Sue asked
Jenny. "I hope you are still seeing him?"

Jenny smiled smugly, as if laughing at a secret joke.

"Adam's working. He should be here soon though."

Star leaned forward and whispered loudly.

"It's not too late, niece! I still think you should go for
Jason."

Jason looked up from the grill just then and caught

Jenny's eye. He gave her a wide smile that reached the corners of his ears. Jenny knew Adam never smiled like that.

"It's too late for a summer wedding," Heather complained, flipping through a wedding magazine. "Stop trying our patience, Jenny."

Jenny went up to the grill and started loading plates with the meat. A side table was loaded with side dishes everyone had brought. Molly had made her brownies and Betty Sue had made bread and butter pudding using a two hundred year old family recipe.

Jenny loaded her plate with coleslaw, potato salad and a bean salad and squirted mustard and relish on her hot dog. She urged everyone to start eating.

Jenny had just taken a bite of her food when Adam arrived, looking tall and handsome in his sheriff's uniform. He made a beeline for the food. The friends talked and laughed together as they enjoyed the food and the company.

Finally, after the second helping of dessert had been eaten and everyone was sitting back, groaning and holding their stomachs, Adam cleared his throat.

He took Jenny's hand and gave her a nod.

"We have an announcement," Jenny began.

"It's about time," Heather cried.

"Just say when," Star added enthusiastically.

"Fall," Jenny said shyly. "We are having an autumn wedding."

***THE END***

Thank you for reading this book. If you enjoyed this book, please consider leaving a brief review. Even a few words or a line or two will do.

As an indie author, I rely on reviews to spread the word about my book. Your assistance will be very helpful and greatly appreciated.

I would also really appreciate it if you tell your friends and family about the book. Word of mouth is an author's best friend, and it will be of immense help to me.

Many Thanks!

Author Leena Clover

http://leenaclover.com

Leenaclover@gmail.com

http://twitter.com/leenaclover

https://www.facebook.com/leenaclovercozymyst erybooks

# Other books by Leena Clover

**Pelican Cove Cozy Mystery Series –**

Strawberries and Strangers

Cupcakes and Celebrities

Berries and Birthdays

Sprinkles and Skeletons

Waffles and Weekends

Parfaits and Paramours

**Meera Patel Cozy Mystery Series -**

Gone with the Wings

A Pocket Full of Pie

For a Few Dumplings More

Back to the Fajitas

Christmas with the Franks

# Acknowledgements

This book would not have been possible without the support of many people. I am thankful to my beta readers and advanced readers and all my loved ones who provide constant support and encouragement. A big thank you to my readers who take the time to write reviews or write to me with their comments – their feedback spurs me on to keep writing more books.

# Join my Newsletter

Get access to exclusive bonus content, sneak peeks, giveaways and much more. Also get a chance to join my exclusive ARC group, the people who get first dibs on all my new books.

Sign up at the following link and join the fun.

Click here →
http://www.subscribepage.com/leenaclovernl

I love to hear from my readers, so please feel free to connect with me at any of the following places.

Website – http://leenaclover.com

Twitter – https://twitter.com/leenaclover

Facebook – http://facebook.com/leenaclovercozymysterybooks

Email – leenaclover@gmail.com

Made in the USA
Coppell, TX
28 June 2022

79332147R00156